A superb work of *fantasy...*
speculative fiction at its finest

Inside, not all is what it seems.
Inside these covers, seven men and women privately
encounter one thing in a uniquely powerful experience: music.

For a teacher of autistic students, a startling revelation comes in
the midst of the mundane. For an ordinary librarian, it's a dream
of dangerous intensity that visits while she sleeps—and later
when she's wide awake, threatening the destruction of what she
holds most dear. For a secondhand store shopper, the sprinkling
tune of a music box invokes a past that's all too personal and
unendurably real... and not quite historically correct. For an
elderly woman in a train station, meanwhile, visions travel the
other direction, coming without warning and horribly, without
mercy. For a retiree, it's a language no human can read. For a
professor, it's nothing less than an epiphany, the answer to the
universe—but he has no way to record it and only minutes before his life fades. For a violin-maker's apprentice, it's a mystery
that can never be solved, only escaped.

From World Fantasy Award winner Zoran Živković comes
Seven Touches of Music, a masterpiece of the mind.

Is *your* life... what it seems?

Accolades

"Živković's work is marked by a quiet and graceful style... by an interest in time, in the effects of knowledge of the future and the past on people's lives, and by a pronounced tendency toward metafictional effects.

"Zoran Živković is revealed here as one of the more interesting voices in contemporary [speculative fiction]."

Locus Magazine

"There is something haunting about these tales, beyond the occult or surreal experiences of the narratives' characters, or the wistful solitude of their existence.

"Meditations, each story possesses the whispered longing and apprehension of a prayer. Reiterative in their elements, these narratives quietly succeed through a compression of language and imagery and a concision of language that should never be overlooked. Phrases within one story inform what will follow in another and, similar to the vibrations of a stringed instrument, create resonances that will echo throughout each story, to be replayed, if faintly and from a differing score, over and over again."

SF Site

"Teasing and clever, fantastical, witty and dark, [Živković's works] get the reader thinking but wear their deep themes lightly; they are mysterious, sometimes even enigmatic, but always accessible.

"Živković's fiction is, above all, always readable, always entertaining. To read these books in succession is akin to dreaming a sequence of vivid dreams, from which one awakes with a heightened perception of life's beauty and strangeness."

Infinity Plus

Seven Touches of Music

a mosaic novel

Zoran Živković

translated from the Serbian
by Alice Copple-Tošić

aio
Aio Publishing Company, LLC

Published by Aio Publishing Company, LLC.

This book is printed on acid-free, recycled paper.

LIBRARY OF CONGRESS CATALOGING-IN-PUBLICATION DATA
Živković, Zoran.
  [Sedam dodira muzike. English]
  Seven touches of music : a mosaic novel / Zoran Živković ; translated from
the Serbian by Alice Copple-Tošić.
    p. cm.
  Includes bibliographical references and index.
  ISBN 1-933083-04-2 (hardcover : alk. paper)
  I. Tošić, Alice. II. Title.

PG1419.36.I954S4313 2006
891.8'236--dc22

      2006003923

Printed and bound in the United States of America.

To Nikola Milošević,
in the name of debts that can never be repaid.

Contents

1. The Whisper

2. The Fire

3. The Cat

4. The Waiting Room

5. The Puzzle

6. The Violinist

7. The Violin-Maker

the whisper

I

It was a small class. And a special one.

There were only five youngsters, three girls and two boys, their ages ranging from six to eleven. Dr. Martin had his hands full with them, but in one respect at least they gave him no worries: he had no need to discipline them. Peace reigned unchallenged in the classroom. It was so quiet that at times Dr. Martin actually longed for a little commotion, some kind of unruly unrest. But all he received from his wards was silence.

They sat silently at their low desks, physically present but mentally absent, detached—worse than that: unattached. They were wrapped in an almost impenetrable autistic shell—certainly one with no shortcut leading through it. Were there a path, to trace it would require endless patience, heroic kindness and attention on a grand scale—not that even these could guarantee success.

Although he liked to regard himself as a teacher, Dr. Martin was truly no such thing. He never taught his pupils anything; nor did he test them, or even talk to them. He did address them, of course, but he could never be certain that they took in any of his words. There was rarely any reaction; when there was, it was enigmatic.

Even so, something was emanating from those five closed, inaccessible worlds. It was hard to understand, but at least it existed. When Dr. Martin had first given the children blank sheets of paper and pencils, he had done so with no great expectations. It was simply part of the standard program. First he had shown them how to use the pencils, which took a wearisome time. Even more time and persistence had been required to persuade them to use them for spontaneous self-expression. The final result was certainly disproportionate to the effort it had cost, but this was true of every aspect of work with these children.

Ana, the oldest but also the smallest in the group, with a face dominated by extremely large eyes, was the first to master the skill of freestyle drawing on paper. She held the pencil in a white-knuckled grip, but her movements were quick, short and nimble. She filled sheet after sheet, but Dr. Martin never saw any of her productions. Should he approach her as she drew her densely cross-hatched lines, she would quickly turn the paper over to prevent him from looking at it. When she decided that a drawing was finished, she would start to tear it up. She did this with geometric precision, first in half, then in quarters, and so on until her desk was piled with tiny squares of gray confetti. These she would carefully sweep into the pocket of her smock, taking them with her at the end of class. Dr. Martin never learned what she did with them.

Sofia was a plump nine-year-old with a round, pimply face which she bent over the desktop because she was very near-sighted. She drew only on the edges of the paper, leaving the middle untouched. She filled this narrow frame with curving lines of surprising accuracy. There were snaking waves, spirals and open loops that never crossed or touched each other, creating a complicated tangle reminiscent of fingerprints. She would interrupt her work occasionally and stare for a long time at what she had drawn. In the end she would hand her work to Dr. Martin with a grimace in which he thought he recognized a shy smile.

Alex, a tall, thin ten-year-old with unruly hair and glasses that were usually halfway down his nose, didn't draw anything. He scribbled haphazardly over the paper with broad, nervous movements until there was not the least bit of white left. Then he would turn the paper over and continue on the other side. The sides of his hands were constantly smudged with graphite, and he often broke his pencil. Once filled, the papers no longer interested him. He would push them away or crumple them up and throw them on the floor. He paid no attention when Dr. Martin came to retrieve them.

Maria was a dark-skinned, slightly cross-eyed girl of eight

with a harelip. She always flinched when Dr. Martin gently addressed her, and never changed her piece of paper. From the beginning she had drawn a complicated design in which a certain regularity could be discerned, although nothing was recognizable. She worked slowly, spending considerable time on details which she constantly embellished while adding new ones. Sometimes she would mutter, quietly and inarticulately, as if talking to someone in the drawing only she could see. During the two months that the drawing class had lasted, she had filled barely half of her first sheet of paper.

Philip, the youngest pupil in the class, had weak capillaries in his nose, so from time to time his nose would bleed spontaneously. If Dr. Martin was slow to notice this, a red spot would spread over the paper in front of the boy. Philip was not bothered by the blood and paid no attention to it; he was completely devoted to his unvarying work of drawing endless rows of little circles on both sides of the paper. His hand was unsteady so the rows were rarely horizontal, and the little circles would gradually get smaller or larger, often distorting into ovals. He would put the completed sheets on the side of his desk next to the blank sheets, paying no attention to Dr. Martin should he take any of them away.

The drawing program did not call for music, but did not preclude it either. Dr. Martin reached gratefully for the idea, once it occurred to him, as relief from the oppressive silence to which he never could acclimatize. There could surely be no

20

harm in some quiet but tuneful composition. It might even have an invigorating effect on his pupils. One never knew—although, of course, one should never allow one's hopes to become too buoyant.

The choice was biased. Dr. Martin brought his favorite CD from home: Chopin's Piano Concerto No. 2 in F Minor, Opus 21. It had the effect of a sedative, though not in the least like those that rendered you numb and insensitive; rather it was calming, making one tranquil and receptive to those vibrations of reality that one might easily miss in an ordinary mood.

When he listened to Chopin alone at home, Dr. Martin always closed his eyes. That would have been inappropriate here in the classroom, but a twinge of disappointment got the better of him. He watched the children for a few moments after the concerto started, secretly hoping for some sort of sign they were at least aware of the sound of the piano and orchestra, but there was none. The five youngsters sat there, engrossed in their usual drawing as if their ears had been plugged with wax, as if completely untouched by the harmony that so enchanted their teacher. Dr. Martin had been plagued by doubts about his work before; there had been moments when it seemed fundamentally futile. But he had never before plumbed the depths of such despair. He closed his eyes to remove himself from the scene, if only for a moment.

The first movement, Maestoso, was already well under way by the time the music at last suppressed the rising tide of bitterness within him. He realized he was actually being unfair to his unfortunate wards. He had greatly overestimated them. Of course they were insensitive to Chopin, just as they were to many other, far less complex joys freely available in the world from which they had withdrawn. It could not be otherwise, as he should have known. He should not have expected miracles.

He opened his eyes and looked at the children in front of him. There was no change: the same bodily positions, the same movements of five pencils on paper. He put out his hand to turn off the stereo. He could have let the concerto play to the end, since it wasn't bothering anyone, but it suddenly seemed senseless for him to go on listening to it by himself. Yet his finger never reached the stop button; just then he noticed that there had been a change after all. And he was to blame. Had he not closed his eyes, irrationally and improperly, for several minutes, he would have noticed Philip's nosebleed.

By the time his rapid strides brought him to the boy, almost one-third of the sheet, tirelessly filled with little circles, was stained with red. It was a distressing sight though it represented no real danger. The bleeding could easily be staunched by inserting a piece pulled from a cotton-wool ball into Philip's left nostril, and Dr. Martin always kept a supply at hand with just that in mind. The young boy did not object. He obediently put his head back, as so many times before, and patiently awaited what came next.

After wiping Philip's mouth and chin with a tissue and mopping up the remains of the gushing blood, Dr. Martin picked up the damp paper and wiped off the desktop with another cotton ball. Then he took a new sheet from the pile in the corner and put it in front of the boy. He was just about to crumple up the paper and throw it away when his eyes strayed briefly to what was written on it. The red film covered something that should not have been there at all.

Dr. Martin had never even tried to teach his young pupil how to write numbers. It simply would not have been worth it. Even normal six-year-old boys have trouble with them, and it was out of the question for autistic children of that age. Nonetheless, here was a long row of numbers, covered by the blood from his nosebleed. There was no interruption to set them apart. The circles suddenly stopped and numbers appeared in their place. Three rows of numbers once again gave way to little circles, except that now they all looked like zeroes. The numbers were not written very skilfully either, but they were easy to recognize even so.

Dr. Martin looked with amazement at the boy, but he was once again absorbed in his endless drawing of round shapes as if nothing unusual had happened. The doctor stood over the boy for a moment, holding the sheet of paper which was starting to curl from dampness. Then, guided by a sudden thought, he started to check on the other children.

But there was nothing unexpected there. Ana, as usual, turned over her paper when he got close, with a reproachful, sidelong glance. Sofia stopped her slow drawing of a thin, sinusoidal line along the very edge of the paper, raised her head and smiled at him, more with her eyes than her mouth. Alex was making broad sweeps on the paper, scribbling with his already blunt pencil, completely indifferent to Dr. Martin's scrutiny. Finally, Maria first flinched a little when he came up, then shyly returned to the details of a design that vaguely resembled a bird with an oversized beak.

Returning to his desk, Dr. Martin reached for the stereo again, but once more changed his mind at the last moment and left it on, although he could not have said why. The Maestoso ended and the second movement began: Larghetto. He placed the sheet of paper he had brought in front of him on the desk and stared at it while the music wrapped him in its spidery web.

A little later he took a blank piece of paper and copied over Philip's three rows of numbers, then put the original in a drawer. There were thirty-two of them, and they seemed to be strung together quite randomly—at least he could discern no pattern, but numbers had never been his strong suit. Maybe someone more skilled in mathematics could make some sense out of them, although he thought not. The very fact that the numbers existed was inexplicable enough. Anything more would be a true miracle.

As a sober man, Dr. Martin did not believe in miracles; nonetheless, after class ended that day he emailed a mathematician friend with the list of thirty-two digits from the blood-stained paper, asking whether they might mean something. He was certain of receiving a negative answer, but still he needed confirmation. As he waited, he felt like someone who, in spite of being completely healthy, is mildly anxious regarding the results of a recent medical checkup.

Two hours later he received a reply.

> *Dear Martin,*
>
> *It didn't take me long to figure out this was a trick question. The problem has nothing to do with mathematics, of course. The series has no numerical pattern, but it has great meaning in physics—at least, the first nine digits have. If you put a decimal point two places before the first seven, then you get 0.00729735308, which is one of the fundamental values of nature, the fine-structure constant. I don't know about the digits after the eight. If they weren't given at random, to confuse me even more, then it must be God himself who whispered them to you because at this moment only He is able to measure after the eleventh significant figure.*
>
> *You surprised me, I must admit. I had no idea you were interested in theoretical physics. Working with handicapped children must be boring you rigid, if you have to seek refuge in riddles like this. Try thinking up something harder next time!*
>
> *Isaac*

Dr. Martin thanked his friend for his swift reply. He praised his quick intuition, and admitted contritely that he was, indeed, a bit bored. Of course the numbers after the eight were arbitrary. How could it be otherwise? He had certainly underestimated Isaac in thinking they could have fooled him.

Dr. Martin's conscience caused him not a twinge for hiding the truth in this way. At present it was out of the question to reveal the true origin of the numbers. He would be obliged to offer some sort of explanation, which he was not prepared to do for a number of reasons, principally that Philip would be exposed to unnecessary unpleasantness thereby. The boy's wellbeing came first, and he would be unable to withstand a multitude of strangers wanting to examine him. He would only withdraw more deeply into himself, making the whole exercise pointless. If anyone was to get involved in the matter, there could be no one more suitable than Dr. Martin himself! There would be time for others later, should that prove necessary or desirable.

He first had to establish what had brought the boy to stop drawing little circles all of a sudden. If that impetus had come from the outside world, then it must have been the music. Nothing else had interrupted the daily routine in class.

Once again Dr. Martin brought the CD with Chopin's second piano concerto and played it at the same volume as before. This time he didn't close his eyes. He watched Philip carefully, but nothing happened. The uniform row of zeroes did not change into anything else. The same happened when

Dr. Martin sat through the whole first movement with his eyes tightly closed, feeling rather idiotic as he did so. He had never been tolerant of actions based on superstition.

Then he considered trying a new composition. For all he knew, the piano concerto worked only once. This assumption did not sound very rational, but he had little choice other than to give it all up. Of course he could not do that! He brought his large collection of CDs into the classroom and started to play them one by one.

Nothing had any further effect on Philip, but there were some unexpected influences on the other children. During Ravel's Suite No. 1, 'Daphnis and Chloe', Ana started to tear her completed drawings into long, thin strips instead of tiny squares. Bach's Toccata and Fugue in D Minor brought tears to Sofia's near-sighted eyes, but also a sort of coughing that resembled a throaty laugh. During Mozart's Symphony No. 40 in G Minor, Alex picked up a pile of scribbled papers and put them neatly on the side of his desk. Finally, at the sound of Debussy's Nocturne, Maria failed to flinch when Dr. Martin came up to her.

All this could have been pure coincidence, of course; Dr. Martin had no time to check it out because his attention was completely focussed on Philip. When he had exhausted his own collection of CDs, he briefly thought of borrowing or buying some others in order to continue the experiment, but thought better of it. He realized it was senseless, since he could go on like that forever. No, he should not have gone beyond Chopin.

The second concerto was of utmost importance, but not just the concerto. There had been something else. But what? And then it dawned on him. The blood, of course! Philip's nose had bled!

This was something he could not precipitate. He had to be patient, but he knew from experience that he would not have to wait long. The boy's weak capillaries broke once every two weeks or so. He had to be ready the next time it happened. He continued his normal work, but often looked in the little boy's direction, waiting for the thin red stream to flow from his left nostril.

When this finally happened, he reacted at once. He pressed the button on the readied player, and the classroom was suddenly filled with resounding piano music. Then he went up to Philip, squatted down next to him and watched him fixedly. The flow of blood first went over the double curve of his lips and then made a winding cut across half his chin. The boy did not stop, even when red petals started to blossom about the paper in front of him. The irregular circles came steadily, one after another, not changing into digits, while a damp red veil spread over them.

It was only when blood had covered a good half of the paper that Dr. Martin finally snapped out of his trance. He leaned the boy's head back with trembling movements and applied a large, white cotton ball to his nostril. All this had been not only senseless, but extremely unkind to Philip. A doctor, of all people, should be the last person to show such cruelty toward the boy!

As he wiped Philip's face with a tissue, he felt his conscience prick him with an almost physical pain.

Dr. Martin went back to his desk and turned off the stereo. The room sank into silence, but no one paid any attention. He should not have played the music, not only because it was superfluous here, but because it had brought nothing but trouble. There had been even less reason to make a second attempt to penetrate something that was clearly way beyond him. If it truly had been a whisper, as Isaac had said in jest, then it had certainly not been intended for his ears.

Moreover, Dr. Martin was just an ordinary specialist in autistic children. His main obligation in that capacity was to protect his wards. The best he could do for Philip at this moment was to forget the whole incident, to pretend that nothing had happened. This wouldn't be hard to do as there was only one trace of evidence, which would be easy to remove.

Dr. Martin opened his desk drawer. He took out the sheet of paper whose wrinkled third had long since lost its bright red color and turned dark brown. With slow movements he tore it into very tiny pieces. They were not as uniform as Ana's confetti, but they too ended up in a pocket, soon to be discarded in a place where no one would ever find them.

the fire

2

Mrs. Martha woke suddenly, jerking up on her elbows. But that did not immediately dispel the dream; it lingered a while, like a frightful echo. At least, the sound did. The image quickly dissolved from under her lowered eyelids into the darkness of the bedroom, but her ears were still filled with music. It was so powerful, it certainly should have wakened Constantine, even though he was a very sound sleeper. But her husband's large shape remained immobile. He was lying on his side with his back to her, like a dark landmass. She stared at him in bewilderment, slowly waking up as the music started to fade, giving way to his deep, noisy breathing, on the edge of snoring.

She looked around, still confused, feeling her heart thud hollowly in her breast. It must be quite early. The large rectangular window was filled with a mute, pre-dawn grayness. From somewhere outside came the barking of a dog, and another more distant bark came in reply. She turned to the bedside table. The large, bright yellow numbers on the alarm clock read 4:47. She squinted at them for several moments, then got up, searched around her bed for her slippers and headed for the bathroom, tottering a little.

She drained a large glassful of water. As she drank the last gulps she realized it was not what she wanted. She wasn't the least bit thirsty. As she lowered the glass to the washstand she caught her reflection in the mirror, and she stared at her face in the striplights, filled with disbelief, as though looking at some stranger rather than herself. Finally she shook her head, turned off the light and went back to bed.

It was going to be hard to get back to sleep, which was a nuisance because she would feel sleepy and out of sorts all day long; but on balance she was glad, because she didn't feel at all like returning to that dream. The dream, however, was inescapable. Lying on her back with the covers pulled up to her chin, staring at the ceiling where pale stripes had started to appear, she tried to concentrate on something ordinary, something innocuous, that would calm her. But her thoughts would not obey her. Something seemed to be pulling them, taking them back to the dream.

She was standing in the middle of a vast, sandy wilderness. Low on the horizon, the sun wrapped the sand in a reddish veil. A gentle breeze was raising little whirlwinds that danced around her bare feet, tickling between her toes. She was wearing a loose, long-sleeved, calf-length white dress resembling Bedouin garb. She felt comfortable in it, though the fabric was rough.

Suddenly she heard the sound of waves, faint but quite recognizable. She turned inquisitively but could not see the sea as she had hoped. Instead, she caught sight of a lone hill behind her. It resembled the shell of a giant turtle that had dragged itself up to end its days in the desert. A huge stone building—a temple, perhaps?—stood on its flat top, like some sort of cubical hump, surrounded by a row of stumpy columns.

A procession was slowly making its way up the left curve of the hill toward the temple. Tall figures wearing robes similar to hers, but dark brown in color and with hoods raised, stood out sharply against the deep blue afternoon sky. Each of them carried an object she did not at once recognize. At first she thought they were a detachment of soldiers carrying strange weapons of various shapes and sizes, but when she looked more closely she saw that they were actually carrying musical instruments. The musicians were on their way to the temple, probably to give a concert there.

How wonderfully propitious! Constantine, unlike herself, was not an admirer of serious music, so they rarely went to concerts. Here was a chance to make up a little for what she had missed, since he, for some reason, was nowhere in sight. She rushed toward the hill, her feet sinking ankle-deep now and then in the soft sand. When she reached the bottom of the hill, the last of the musicians were disappearing into the temple. The slope was not gentle, but she climbed effortlessly, feeling the smooth, warm stones under her feet.

On reaching the top a surprise awaited her. There was no door where she was sure she had seen the musicians entering the building. Instead there was a flat yellow wall of massive stone blocks, faded from long exposure to the sun. An inscription was written across the four columns spaced along the entire lateral façade, but she was unable to read it as she didn't know Greek.

Seeking the entrance, she rushed to the right along a cobbled path. She went all around the rectangular temple but could find no opening except for a row of slits at the very top of the long sides of the building, probably serving to admit light. Certainly, only a bird could enter there. Returning to her starting point she stopped in confusion, not knowing what to do. The concert might start at any moment and she was very keen not to miss it.

As if to confirm her apprehensions, music started to pour out of the temple. It came from high up, probably through the illumination holes. At first she was frustrated at having been unable to enter the building in time, but then, quite unexpectedly, another feeling displaced her exasperation. Her soul was filled with anxiety, although she didn't understand what was causing it. The sounds from inside grew steadily louder over several long moments before she realized they were actually what was upsetting her.

There was something deranged about the sounds. She couldn't determine exactly what it was, but she was overcome by a strange certainty that something in addition to music was issuing from the instruments of those hooded figures who had magically passed into the doorless temple. Whatever it was, it was as intangible as the sounds, but by no means innocuous. Spurred by a dark premonition, she ran toward the long side of the building. One look at the illumination slits was enough to confirm her fears. Tongues of flame were darting from the narrow windows.

Panic seized her. The fire could not harm the thick stone walls, but something much more flammable was inside the building, and it was now in danger. She did not wonder what it might be, nor how she knew of it—none of that mattered now, and she could think about it later. First she had to find a way to put out the blaze. She was the only one available to do it.

Yes, but how? She set her mind feverishly to work, biting her lower lip as she always did in times of great tension. She needed water. Where could she find water in the desert? And then she remembered the waves she had heard while down in the flatland. A quick survey of the terrain surrounding the hilltop was enough; there, indeed, was the sea, its blue surface dotted with crests of foamy white.

It wasn't far, just a short walk away, but for her needs the sea might as well have been infinitely distant. Even had the temple been built right on the shore, there was nothing she could do. How would she carry the water to extinguish the fire? All she had were her cupped hands.

As if mocking her helplessness, the music and the fire grew louder and stronger. Flames were now flickering wildly out of the openings at the top of the wall, forcing her to step back from the heat to the very edge of the hill's flat summit. The music had grown so loud she was forced to place her hands over her ears. It was of little avail. The ground around her soon began to shake, evidently from the force of the vibrations, at first slowly and then with greater and greater intensity, as if in the grip of an earthquake. She lost her balance for a moment and fell to her hands and knees, but managed to avoid plunging down the hillside.

She was filled with horror as she saw that even the stone temple could not resist the destructive impact of the music. Completely deafened, she watched mesmerized as the columns swayed and toppled into cylindrical segments. One of them started to roll toward her, but all she could do was stare at it, unable to move. It passed so close it almost grazed her, then continued down the steep slope, picking up speed as it went.

For a moment she hoped it was all over; then the heavy stone roof collapsed into the interior of the building with a tremendous crash. Pandemonium ensued. She felt not the slightest compassion for the musicians, who were presumably crushed beneath. It served them right. It was all their fault! Without their demonic music none of this would have happened. But the music didn't stop. It could still be heard rising from the fiery ruins, even louder now that there was no roof to dampen the sound; the collapse had hindered the musicians not in the slightest.

The fire now reached high into the sky. She was overcome with deep despair when it became clear there was no way to save the delicate, fragile thing somewhere inside. She still didn't know what it was, but nothing could survive such infernal conflagration. It had been lost, inexorably and forever, leaving behind an emptiness as gaping as the tomb. She had not been able to do a thing, and now it was too late.

It was also too late for her to get away. The wall, with its large *stone blocks, started to swell like an inflatable balloon. Only a few more moments and it would yield before the unimaginable pressure from within. Suddenly she realized she had no shelter. There was not even time to flee headlong down the hillside. All she managed to do, as the sounds rushed inexorably toward their demented crescendo, was to raise her hands instinctively to her face and close her eyes tight. Darkness swallowed the terrifying sight, but nothing was able to banish the final explosion of music.*

Mrs. Martha did manage to fall asleep again, but not until broad daylight. This time there were no dreams. She simply sank into a lake of black ink that absorbed her into its blind, deaf sanctuary. She could have stayed there a very long time, but Constantine didn't let her. He reached for her, gently shook her shoulder, and pulled her to the surface. She tried to resist, not wanting to emerge, but he was merciless.

Her dream remained behind in the inky lake. She hadn't the slightest memory of it after waking up the second time that morning. When her husband asked why she had overslept, she answered with a shrug. It seemed odd to her, too. She was usually the first one out of bed. She was vaguely aware of some sort of anxiety, but even though she tried to discover its cause, it remained unfathomable.

At breakfast, when Constantine put slices of fresh toast on the table, she glanced with hostility at the striped surface. She liked toast, but for some reason didn't feel like any today. Her husband gave her an inquiring look, seeing her push the empty plate away, but said nothing. She drank a full cup of coffee, blowing at it even though it wasn't hot. She knew she would have trouble with it on an empty stomach, but still wasn't able to eat a thing.

When they left for work, Constantine turned on the car radio. He had been doing this regularly for a long time, although he wasn't very interested in music. It was the best way to alleviate the strained silence that would otherwise engulf them during the half-hour ride. After more than twenty years of living together they were running out of topics for conversation. This had bothered her at first, but later she had got used to it, and even come to like it. Better to talk when they had a genuine reason rather than by the dictates of convention. She, too, was not always in a mood to talk.

Now, however, her hand extended itself; first she turned the music down, despite the fact that it wasn't loud, then she turned it altogether off. She said nothing while doing so, and when she had done it she couldn't have said why. The radio was tuned to a station specializing in light instrumental music, one she had always enjoyed before. This morning it seemed somehow irritating, although she would not have been able to give the reason. Constantine turned his head briefly toward her. She endured his inquisitive look, thankful that he did not ask her anything. They continued driving in silence, the traffic around them growing denser as they approached the city center. When they got close to the library where she worked, her attention was drawn to something she would probably not have noticed previously. Two fire trucks were trying without success to make their way through the multitude of cars inching forward in the morning rush-hour traffic. Their sirens were blaring and their blue lights flashed, but to little effect. The cars in front of them simply had nowhere to go to let them pass.

Mrs. Martha became suddenly anxious and started to breathe rapidly, as she always did in that state. The thought that the huge red vehicles might not get where they were needed in time filled her with unusual discomfort. She had no idea where the fire had broken out, but that did not seem to matter. Regardless of what was burning, the damage would be enormous. Fire left an utter wasteland behind it, and this might be threatening something truly unique, something that could never be recreated.

The fire trucks turned left at the first intersection and drove out of sight. Their sirens could still be heard for a while, until they were gradually drowned out by the surrounding noise. As though emerging from a daze, Mrs. Martha wondered confusedly why this was having such an effect on her. Fires happened every day in large cities such as this. It was inevitable—just as it was inevitable that many people ended their lives daily, people who were also unique and could never be recreated. But one should not allow oneself to be overly burdened with the irretrievable losses of every day; that would turn life into a real inferno.

Before she got out of the car in front of the library, Mrs. Martha kissed Constantine—just a light touch of the lips that seemed barely more intimate than a handshake. They didn't say anything to each other; there was no need. He would drive on as he did every morning to the insurance company where he had worked for almost a quarter of a century. At the end of the working day he would wait for her at this same spot. Then they would kiss again, without a word. The radio would already be on in the car, freeing both of them from the obligation to talk about the arid monotony of their daily working lives.

As soon as she turned on the computer in her office, as she did each morning, she realized something was wrong. A picture appeared immediately on the screen. That should not have happened; it always took about half a minute for the system to boot up. During that time a rapid sequence of vertical text filled with sundry abbreviations, signs and numbers would pass across the screen. They moved far too fast for her to read and their meaning had never interested her; she understood very little about computers. She could find her way around the basic library program, and that was quite enough for her. She hadn't the slightest desire to learn in more detail how the thing worked.

Now it looked as if she had turned on a television set. The picture was not the computer's usual coarse representation, which she had never liked; it was a very high resolution picture of the outside of an ancient building. She stared at it in confusion. It seemed vaguely familiar, yet she could not recall where she had seen it before. Four large columns ran at regular intervals along the façade, and between the two at the center stood an imposing rectangular entrance, its double doors wide open.

Above the columns was some sort of inscription. She moved her head a bit closer to the screen to get a better look, but this was not necessary. As if in response to her wishes, the camera started to zoom in on the carved letters. The letters were in Greek, but still she managed to read them. For some reason this did not surprise her very much. It was certainly the lesser of the two wonders confronting her just then. The second had to do with the inscription itself. Although it was most certainly impossible, she could nonetheless clearly read: Great Library.

She stared in momentary disbelief at the letters. Then she came to her senses, realizing she should do something. She had to call someone—maybe the computer maintenance department. This was certainly some kind of breakdown. These machines went on the blink from time to time, although she had never heard of anything like this before. She reached for the telephone, but didn't finish because that same moment the camera came back to life. It glided down from the inscription, went to the open door and floated inside.

Not much could be seen at first. The only light came from a row of slits near the top of the long lateral walls, but this was not enough after the bright sunlight outside. When the picture quickly started to get lighter, Mrs. Martha thought her eyes were becoming accustomed to the gloom, although she knew it was only an illusion. The camera was adjusting to the weak light. Then it began to rotate, slowly revealing the interior.

There was only one large space, resembling a hall. Its central part contained a row of wooden tables surrounded by simple chairs without backs, stretching all the way to the far end. The tables were placed in such a way as to catch the rays of light slanting from the high openings. That was enough to read by without straining one's eyes during the day, particularly if it was sunny. There did not seem to be any artificial light. There were no oil lamps or candles. Nothing that would burn. The Great Library clearly could not be used at night.

All four walls were completely covered with deep shelves from floor to ceiling. Ladders were placed at frequent intervals. These were connected to the shelves, giving access to their upper reaches. There were things on the shelves that Mrs. Martha did not immediately recognize. Having expected books, she stared in bewilderment at the tube-shaped objects that formed a vast honeycomb on all sides.

And then it dawned on her. If the inscription above the entrance were to be believed, there could be no conventional books here. It was too early for bound books. Documents were written on papyrus when this building existed. On the screen in front of her stretched an enormous repository for scrolls. She had never been good at making rough calculations, but she could not be mistaken in this case. Along the walls were thousands and thousands of scrolls.

It was an impressive sight; the first thing that crossed Mrs. Martha's mind when she realized what she was looking at, however, was quite practical. As someone who was proud of her profession of librarian, she couldn't resist wondering how it was possible to find one's way about this multitude when there were not even spines to help distinguish one papyrus from another. How could someone quickly find the desired scroll among the countless others that looked identical?

As if following her thoughts once again, the camera moved up close to one section of a shelf. The screen was now filled with only some fifty scrolls. Suddenly they were covered by a porous network of letters. This time they were in the Roman alphabet so Mrs. Martha no longer had to count on a miracle in order to read them. It also did not take her long to realize what it was all about. After all, she had spent her whole life cataloging books.

Authors' names were written in large yellow letters and under them, in smaller blue letters, were the titles. It wasn't clear whether they referred to the works contained in the few scrolls currently visible in the background, but if this were true then the total contents of the papyrus rolls was significantly greater than she might have guessed. What an incredible treasure was to be found in the Great Library! Mrs. Martha's breath grew shorter for the second time that morning.

The camera glided smoothly to the next section of the shelf. The catalog disappeared, but a new one soon took its place. This time Mrs. Martha concentrated on the text. She combed through her memory but could not recall ever having encountered some of the names written on the screen. She tried from the inventory of works to figure out who the authors might be—literary writers, historiographers, natural scientists, mathematicians—but was not certain of anything.

And then she saw a name she recognized. Her own library had recently received a new edition of his tragedies which she herself had placed upon the shelves. She well remembered that only a small number of this author's works had been preserved, only seven or eight, and yet before her ran a much longer list. She counted thirty-six dramas. Owing to the small size of the letters she had to count by drawing her finger across the screen. When she passed over a title, its light blue color immediately darkened.

Led by a sudden thought, she raised her index finger to the screen again and placed it on one of the titles that did not seem familiar to her. The letters first changed shade, and then a moment later the catalog page disappeared and one of the scrolls began to emerge from the shelf. When it was all the way out, the scroll unrolled, covering the screen completely. Before Mrs. Martha was the original text of a long-lost tragedy.

The instincts of an experienced librarian hushed her mounting excitement. She had to try to do something. That was uppermost in her mind. All the rest could wait for a more suitable moment—all the disturbing questions that were trying to pour out of wherever she had tucked them away for the time being. Yes, but how? What should she do to save this invaluable treasure that had somehow surfaced from the depths of oblivion? She thought it over with care, but all that came to her mind was to resort to the customary way of recording data on the computer. She didn't think it would work, but what else could she do?

The moment she touched the first key on the keyboard, the papyrus scroll rolled back up and returned to its place in the honeycomb. Mrs. Martha jerked her hand back as though scalded. She had made a mistake. There was no opportunity to try anything else because the camera suddenly moved back from the bookshelf and withdrew to the furthest end of the room, high up under the roof; now it showed the entire Great Library, with the brightly lit entrance at the other end.

Nothing moved for several moments, as though the screen held a photograph. And then the speakers, which had been silent until then, came to life. The music they started to emit was barely audible at first, as though coming from outside, from a distance, so she did not recognize it right away. When the volume began to increase, however, Mrs. Martha felt an icy shiver crawl up her spine. Streaming out of the inky lake where it had lain submerged, the forgotten dream slapped her violently in the face. She knew who she would see even before the procession of musicians reached the entrance. Lit from behind, the hooded figures began to slip inside like faceless ghosts, as if not touching the ground. When they left the bright rectangle at the door, they melted completely into the surrounding darkness. Their presence could only be discerned by the unceasing music. When the last musician entered the Great Library, the tall double doors closed soundlessly behind him, leaving no trace that they had existed.

For a while nothing moved again on the almost totally black screen. Coming from now invisible sources, the music rose ominously. Then bright spots started to speckle the deep shadows. Several moments passed before Mrs. Martha realized what was happening. Torches were being lit one by one, gradually illuminating the spacious interior. What these smoking, flickering lights revealed seemed impossible. The torches were floating in mid-air, without any support; no one was holding them. There was no sign of the musicians, though the music still thundered.

Once all the torches were alight, they took up positions evenly distributed around the large building, forming a long rectangle along the walls. Mrs. Martha gripped the edge of the desk in front of her, as if afraid of losing her footing. She stared fixedly at the screen. She was perfectly aware of what was to come, but the powerlessness she had felt in her dream tied her hands in her waking state as well. Although she tried feverishly to think of a way of preventing the inevitable, nothing came to mind.

The torches stood motionless next to the shelves for a moment; then, as if at some inaudible command, commenced their demented feast. Like the flaming paintbrushes of a crazed, many-handed painter, they started to dip and sway over the papyrus background. The huge fresco was covered with flickering, flaming colors. Mrs. Martha bit almost through her lower lip, as though sharp pain could release her from this unwanted dream. But this time no awakening could save her.

She watched in despair as the fiery orgy gobbled up the scrolls one after the other, reducing their invaluable contents to nothingness. Accompanied by the deranged music, the fire quickly gained momentum and finally occupied the screen completely. The image of the raging fire was so convincing that Mrs. Martha thought she could feel its heat on her face. The burning smell that seemed to fill her nostrils was even more intense. And then she saw with horror that this was not just an illusion: somewhere from the back of the monitor rose a ribbon of gray smoke.

She almost jumped off her chair, knocking it over behind her. Her hands flew to her mouth, but not fast enough to suppress the cry that escaped. The smoke in front of her became thicker, then turned reddish, and finally mixed with the flames that started to stream upwards. Mrs. Martha should have known how to cope with such a situation, she had been trained and knew what she must do, but she was completely paralyzed. She stared dully at the fire as it engulfed the whole monitor. By some miracle, the picture was still there, so the two fires now seemed to merge into one, while music still poured out of the speakers.

When water suddenly gushed from above, Mrs. Martha

did not even try to get out of the way. Smoke had activated the sprinkler system and water started to shower from innumerable little holes in the ceiling. She stood under this dense, piercing shower, her eyes still riveted to the screen, by now empty. The speakers were also silent. The room's power supply had automatically shut down the moment the sprinklers started to work. Like every modern library, this one was properly guarded against the greatest threat to books since time immemorial.

Mrs. Martha spent the next two and a half hours wrapped in a blanket in the ladies' room, waiting for her clothes to be dried and ironed. When she returned to her office everything had been wiped up and put in order. She did not have to explain anything. No one even asked her what had happened, since it was quite obvious. Monitors had caught fire before. It was just an unpleasant incident without too much damage. In any case, everything was insured. A new monitor was already waiting on her desk, but she did not turn her computer back on that day.

Late in the afternoon, when she got into the car and kissed Constantine, she was briefly tempted to tell him what had happened, but held back. She would only get mixed up trying to explain something that she herself did not understand. In addition, he was even less in a mood to talk on the way home from work than in the morning. The drained expression on his face clearly said as much. Finally, the radio was already turned on. Without exchanging a single word, they joined the dense flow of traffic.

the cat

3

Mr. Oliver did not start visiting secondhand shops until after the death of his wife. Mrs. Katerina had often visited such places, particularly during her latter years, and would occasionally bring something home, usually an ornament of some kind. He had never accompanied her, though she had often invited him to come along. He had a certain aversion to old things, especially ones that had previously belonged to other people. This was not shared by Mrs. Katerina. She bought whatever she found pretty and not too expensive.

She had bought Oscar in much the same spirit. She had seen him at a pet shop, priced cheap as he was not purebred. The snow-white kitten with chestnut eyes had enchanted Mrs. Katerina at first sight, though Mr. Oliver had greeted Oscar's arrival with reserve. He was certainly not a cat-lover, although he had nothing against them. He would have said he was simply indifferent to cats.

At first he tried to have as little contact as possible with Oscar, considering the attention his wife lavished on the cat quite enough—more than enough, indeed. Sometimes he felt she treated Oscar more like a child than a cat. She took meticulous care of all his needs, kept him neat and fastidiously clean, even gave him his own room, though he spent very little time there. In addition, she talked to the cat a lot, mainly in baby talk, which had aroused some misgivings in Mr. Oliver, though of course he never remarked upon it.

Over time Mr. Oliver and the cat evolved a truce. If they were unable to establish a closer relationship, at least they learned to put up with each other. Mr. Oliver became used to the tomcat's presence in the house and was no longer bothered by his smell, his hair everywhere when he moulted, his habit of sharpening his claws on the upholstery, the compulsion to tear frantically about the house that seized him without warning and for no apparent reason at least once a day, and the agitation that came over him should a lady cat pay a call anywhere nearby.

For his part, Oscar stopped eyeing or sniffing suspiciously at Mr. Oliver, as if at a shady stranger, and was happy to avoid any physical contact with him. Mrs. Katerina tried briefly to bring them closer together, then gave up, seeing the futility of her efforts. She was nonetheless very careful to divide her affection evenly between them so that neither felt deprived.

The relationship between Mr. Oliver and Oscar changed

when Mrs. Katerina first took to her bed, and shortly thereafter went into hospital. Mr. Oliver had to take over the care of the tomcat. At first he had trouble coping and Oscar found it difficult to accept the change. But gradually Mr. Oliver acquired skill in the basic things—preparing food and cleaning up after the cat—and Oscar became less distrustful.

Even so, when Mr. Oliver brushed the cat, although he clearly enjoyed it, he did not purr in response, as he had with Mrs. Katerina. This perturbed Mr. Oliver a little. Trouble also arose when once a month he leashed the cat and took him for a walk in the park, to find the grass that helped his digestion. Mr. Oliver always felt uneasy doing that, sure that many amazed and even reproachful eyes were on him.

But all this was bearable. The only thing Mr. Oliver could not bring himself to do was talk to Oscar. Although he made several attempts, he felt foolish every time, as if he had been caught talking to himself, and fell silent after only a few words. It was even worse when he tried to baby-talk the cat. It seemed hopelessly artificial and affected, as if Mr. Oliver were adopting a persona entirely unsuited to his age.

As if affected by the same diffidence, Oscar meowed less and less. That had been his way of informing Mrs. Katerina of his wishes, but he preferred to convey his needs to Mr. Oliver by scratching, often suffering when this was not noticed in time. The two of them were clearly condemned to mutual silence; their intimacy had reached a point beyond which neither could proceed.

When Mrs. Katerina died, the question of what would become of Oscar was never even raised. It was, of course, out of the question for Mr. Oliver to turn the cat out, even had he wished to do so. Unaccustomed to fending for himself, the cat would not survive very long in the street. Had he wanted to get rid of him, Mr. Oliver would have preferred to consign the cat to a society for the protection of animals, or possibly return him to the store from which he had been bought. But Mr. Oliver did not want this by any means. Without Oscar, he would be left completely alone in the large, empty apartment, and that thought filled him with horror. Perhaps he and the cat did not get along perfectly well, but now they needed each other. In any case, Katerina would never forgive him if he let Oscar go.

Mr. Oliver's guilty conscience pressured him into visiting secondhand shops. Now it was too late, he realized he should not have refused Katerina's invitations to join her. Had he gone, they would have shared many more pleasant moments together. How strange that one only began to value such things when they were beyond reach. He thought briefly of taking Oscar with him, at least occasionally—it seemed somehow fitting. Yet he refrained; animals were probably not allowed in such places, not even on a leash.

At first he shied away from actually entering junk shops. In his inexperience he imagined they must be like other stores, in which eager salespeople immediately accosted you. If that were to happen, he would find himself in an awkward situation, because he wasn't looking for anything in particular. Luckily, however, there was no such pressure. If he were addressed at all it would only be with a polite greeting, after which he would be left to poke around the vast jumble of small and large objects which crammed every available corner for as long as he liked.

His aversion toward old, secondhand things slowly started to fade. Picking at leisure through crowded shelves and glass showcases, he came to see the items on display through the eyes of his late wife: he saw the beauty in them. The age of an object had no effect on it, and his recent experience with death reminded him painfully that any ownership could endure but a short time.

Indeed, how could anyone own beauty? Who actually owned all those decorative little things that Mrs. Katerina had brought home from junk shops over all those years? He did, presumably—but certainly not for long. If they'd had children, he might take another view of the situation, but without heirs he had no way of knowing what would happen to these objects after his death. It made no difference, nor should it. Soon afterwards, when he started to buy things he found pretty, he regarded none of them as his possessions. They would be with him only temporarily. All he had been given was a brief time in which to enjoy them.

He discovered beauty in the widest range of objects: the chipped ceramic figurine of a ballerina, a cracked badge of honor, an incomplete set of tunic buttons, a worn-out brass pipe-stand, a pocket watch with half the big hand missing, a snuffbox whose lid did not close properly, a rusted key which must once have opened an elaborate lock, a small set of lead soldiers with most of the paint chipped off, a wall barometer from which the mercury had leaked, a pile of sundry old coins, cutlery that might have been gilded at one time, a dented thimble inscribed with a Latin motto in cursive script, a bottle of lavender water, now dried out despite its ground-glass stopper, an empty monocle frame, a tea strainer with its handle bent slightly askew, an album partially filled with old, yellowed photographs of people no one would now recognize.

After bringing these things home, he would not immediately put them on the narrow black shelf with its many compartments, made to order for this special purpose. First, according to his wife's habit, he would give Oscar a chance to sniff them thoroughly in order to become acquainted with them; then he would spend long, patient hours at the kitchen table repairing, fixing, gluing, straightening, fastening, sewing, polishing and painting. In time he collected a wide assortment of tiny tools for such purposes and acquired skills he had never before possessed. When each item finally reached the shelf, it was in the best shape it could possibly be. Only once, during an especially tedious undertaking, did he wonder in amazement that the things Katerina had brought from secondhand shops had never needed any refurbishing.

Mr. Oliver came across the music box by accident. He tripped over it, literally, when approaching a glass case in the corner of a junk shop in a suburb he had not previously visited. It was on the floor, partially covered by the long velvet drapes that framed the display window. He bent down and picked it up, fearful that he might have damaged it inadvertently with his foot. As the sudden, dull sound disturbed the silence, the shopkeeper, who had been engrossed in his accounts, stared inquisitively over his small, round glasses at his only customer.

In other circumstances, Mr. Oliver would certainly not have bought the music box. It was too bulky to fit on the shelf in the living room. Worse, he concluded that he did not care for it when he took a closer look. He did not mind that it was quite worn and most likely didn't work; probably he could remedy such defects. But he didn't see the spark of beauty that was crucial to him.

He doubted he had caused any additional damage to the music box when he tripped over it, but the dealer kept looking at him suspiciously, so he had no way out. Disinclined and unprepared to haggle, he simply went up to the counter and asked the price. When he was told, the price clearly included the dealer's experienced appraisal of a customer who was in a bind, but he did not attempt to bargain—he never bargained. He paid the amount without a word and waited for the music box to be wrapped.

A small problem arose in this regard. The shopkeeper,

whose expression had relaxed into a smile once the money was in the cash register, had trouble finding anything large enough to hold the music box. He finally disappeared behind the curtain that covered the entrance to the back of the store and brought out a large cardboard box originally intended for boots. He then saw his esteemed customer out with the bow and broad smile proper to the occasion.

When he got home, Mr. Oliver was still uncertain about what to do with the music box. He could put it away somewhere and forget it, but that made no sense. If he hadn't wanted it, the best thing would have been to chuck it into the first trash can he came across after he left the junk shop. He was certainly not the type to cling tenaciously to old things when they were certain never to be used again. Since he had already brought it home, why not try to fix it up a little? Maybe it would grow on him with time.

He went into the kitchen where he did his repairs, took the music box out of its wrapping and placed it on the table. As Oscar always did when something new was brought home, he came at once to sniff it, jumping first onto the chair and then to the table. Mrs. Katerina would not have allowed this, but Mr. Oliver had relaxed almost all her restrictions. Even when he wanted to prohibit Oscar from doing something, he usually hesitated because he didn't know how to go about it.

Mr. Oliver expected Oscar to go up to the musical device, but for some reason the cardboard box attracted him instead.

He sniffed it carefully all over, then climbed inside, pulling himself under the half-open lid. When the tip of his tail disappeared the lid went down with him, so he was completely enclosed. This did not disturb Mr. Oliver. Oscar often found his way into various inaccessible places and always got out easily, without anyone's help. All he had to do here was rise a little and lift the lid with his head.

There was a bit of scratching and commotion inside and then everything went silent. Oscar was obviously hiding, something cats do when they think they're in a safe environment. He would come out when he got bored. Mr. Oliver returned to the music box. He looked it over carefully, then took a flannel rag and started to clean it. To judge by the thick layer of dust, no one had used it in a long time.

After cleaning the outside, Mr. Oliver grasped the white porcelain handle that wound the device. Quite a bit of effort was needed to turn it. From inside the box came the squeaking of gears and springs that had not been oiled recently. He had to turn the handle very slowly so that nothing inside would get stuck or break. It took him quite a while, but he was in no hurry. Undoubtedly it would take considerable effort to make the music box work, and the question was whether he was equal to such a job. It was one thing to fix up simple objects on the outside, quite another to repair a complex device like this. After all, he was not a mechanical engineer.

He had just decided that nothing would happen when to

his surprise the mechanism started to emit sounds. The music was stiff, scratchy and broken, but he could make out the basic melody. It sounded gay and enthusiastic, with a lively rhythm—a polka, perhaps. Mr. Oliver thought he had heard it somewhere before, but since he had no ear for and little understanding of music, he could not recognize it. But all this suddenly lost importance when the lid of the boot box at the other end of the table started to rise.

The head that appeared was not Oscar's. It seemed somehow smaller, more like that of a female cat than a tomcat; in addition there was not a single white hair on it. Gray, brown and black colors competed discordantly for supremacy, and jade-green eyes stood out against this mainly dark background. The cat examined her surroundings inquisitively for several moments, showing no interest whatsoever in the fixed stare of Mr. Oliver, either accepting his presence as part of the furniture or not noticing him at all.

Then she slipped out from under the lid and onto the table. The cat looked about the kitchen briefly, stretched after being cramped in the box, and jumped first onto the chair and thence to the floor. Mr. Oliver watched her without moving as she headed toward the dining room. He had the impression that she brushed against his leg as she passed him, but he hadn't felt any touch, probably because of the confused state he was in. The cat moved lithely, like Oscar, though somehow in a softer and more feminine manner. With brisk steps she soon reached the door which stood ajar and disappeared into the next room.

Mr. Oliver hesitated several seconds before starting after her. He was beset by the desire to peer into the boot box to see what had happened to Oscar. He didn't do so; not only because it was not the most important thing at the moment but also because he shuddered at what he might see if he lifted the lid. Instead he headed toward the dining room, pursued by lively sounds from the music box. He did not open the door all the way when he reached it, though he already had his hand on the doorknob. He stopped in front of it, for from the other side came something that positively should not have been there: the murmur of voices.

He tried to identify them, but the piercing music behind his back interfered. Several people were talking at the same time, and the squeaky, clamorous voices of children and their noisy laughter rose above the rest. Mr. Oliver stared at the door in front of him, bewildered, not knowing what to do. The reasonable part of his mind told him to open the door and find out what was going on in the dining room. But another part, deeply hidden, feverishly held him back, insisting the contrary: that he close the door at once, by no means look inside, get away as soon as possible, even flee.

When he finally started to open the door, slowly and hesitantly, he did so only because he believed he would never forgive himself if he didn't do so. In addition, something in the indistinct voices from the dining room was calming, and even more than that: familiar. He could not determine exactly what it was, but what he felt was enough to convince him that nothing bad would happen.

In the dining room he found the oval table laid for lunch. Five chairs were occupied with two adults and three children sitting and eating. It was a family meal, its atmosphere gay and relaxed because there were no guests whose presence would require formal behavior. Not a single head turned toward the uninvited visitor standing in astonished confusion at the kitchen door. He stayed there, immobile, like an invisible ghost.

His eyes first stopped on Katerina. He had some pictures of her from when she was young, of course, but the only place she remained as lively as she looked now was in his memory, although he couldn't remember her hair like this. Next to her was the youngest of the three children, a little girl with freckles and long, dark, curly locks wearing a stained bib. Her mother repeatedly lifted spoonfuls of soup from a bowl, saying each time that it wasn't hot as she blew unnecessarily on the thick, red liquid, while the little girl tried, through a babbling string of words, to postpone the inevitable as long as possible.

The boys sitting on either side of their father were twins, three or perhaps four years older than their sister. They wore identical clothes and had very short hair. The one on the right was recounting, with a lot of giggling, one of his and his brother's recent larks, trying to keep everyone's attention by raising his voice. He continued to eat all the while, so his father had to quiet him down and remind him not to talk with his mouth full. The other boy was eating in silence, waiting for the chance when no one was watching to drop a bit of food to the tortoise-shell cat standing by his chair.

Feeling a swarm of needles land on the back of his head, Mr. Oliver finally looked at the father. What struck him first was how different he looked with a mustache. At one time, soon after he married, he had started one, but Katerina hadn't been very pleased with it so he had abandoned the idea. Now he concluded it didn't look that bad on him. It lent a certain seriousness to the young face, as befitted the head of the family. The glasses also contributed to this effect, though Mr. Oliver found them less appealing. He was proud his sight was still quite good despite his advanced age.

When Katerina got up, took the soup tureen from the table and headed toward the kitchen, the old man standing at the door, captivated by the impossible sight before him, was startled out of his paralysis. He couldn't just remain there, blocking her way, but what should he do? Complicated questions, which he had suppressed until that moment, started to appear everywhere, finding no answers as the young woman drew inexorably closer.

And then, as if things were not hopeless enough, behind Mr. Oliver's back came a sharp, metallic rattle followed by a high-pitched gasp. His nerves taut, he jerked around, but nothing was happening there. The music box had stopped playing, either because the spring had wound down or—more likely, given the squeaky wheeze that had just echoed—because some part of the neglected mechanism had finally collapsed.

Mr. Oliver quickly turned his head back toward the dining room, expecting to collide with Katerina, but no one was coming toward him any longer. There was no mother carrying a soup tureen. There was no daughter who didn't like hot soup, no son who liked to talk while he ate, no second son who liked to sneak food to the cat. There was no young father with a mustache and glasses heading the table at the family meal. The large room gaped empty and quiet, just as it had for so many years.

Mr. Oliver remained standing at the door to the room, glazed eyes staring, until a new noise came from the kitchen. It was considerably softer, so this time he did not have to turn around so suddenly. Out of the boot box appeared first a whiskered muzzle, then a white head. Oscar stayed like that for a while, as if wondering whether to go back inside his nice hiding place or leave it. Finally the lid rose a bit further and he glided onto the table.

Even before Mr. Oliver reached Oscar, he had come to a decision. He would not be able to repair the music box after all. Better not even to try. It might well not be fixable, and even if it were, the repairs might cost more than the price of a new music box—and in any case, he had no desire to own one. He put it back in the cardboard box, put the box under his arm and left his apartment, followed by Oscar's inquisitive eyes.

When he appeared at the door to the junk shop carrying the box, the owner eyed him suspiciously, sensing trouble. He was just about to tell the customer, with a suitably implacable expression on his face, that items purchased in his store could not be returned (as was clearly stated in the framed sign on the wall) when Mr. Oliver interrupted him with a movement of his hand.

After the shopkeeper found that he was not expected to return the money he had been paid, only to take back the music box without any compensation, he wrinkled his brow briefly, wondering what traps might be lurking behind such a strange offer. Being able to find none, he finally agreed, trying to insinuate by his tone of voice that he was doing so unwillingly and as a special favor. His conviction that he had made a very good deal was only slightly dented when the customer left the shop with the bow and the broad smile of one who has gotten by far the best of the bargain.

Immediately on returning home, Mr. Oliver recounted to Oscar his experiences with the secondhand dealer. The tomcat listened attentively, not interrupting him with superfluous meowing. That would begin to happen somewhat later, as he listened to other stories, restrained and shy at first and then increasingly uninhibited, as the voice of the old man with whom he lived gradually softened, on its way to turning into baby talk.

the waiting room

4

Miss Adele did not like traveling.

She had not enjoyed it much even in her younger days, and as the years passed she found the occasional need to travel ever less agreeable. But she could not avoid this trip, though there was nothing in its favor. First of all it was winter, and one of the harshest to hit the region in a long time, with heavy snowfalls that completely disrupted the rail system. The schedules had become unreliable, as the snowdrifts not only slowed the trains down but often stranded them for hours in the middle of nowhere. Moreover, the general situation was gloomy and tense. Although everyone felt that war would not break out before spring, no one would have been very surprised should it come much sooner.

When Miss Adele received the news that her younger sister, Mrs. Teresa, had taken ill, her first thought was that this was a threefold vexation. She was naturally upset at her sister's illness, which came as a complete surprise, but she found the two necessities resulting from this misfortune almost as irksome. She would certainly have to visit her sister. That, even if everything went well, meant an exhausting five-hour train journey, and in such bad weather the trip's duration might be open-ended. She could already see herself shivering in an unheated compartment, in who knows what kind of company, as the train stood hopelessly trapped in the middle of a gloomy, white wasteland. But even that would be preferable to the meeting that awaited her.

She had never forgiven Teresa for marrying that man and going off with him so far away, leaving her alone. Adele had disliked him at first sight. He was so full of himself, so negative, and cynical as only men know how to be. And then there were those watery eyes of his that looked derisively down at you, and his thick, red beard that smelled of tobacco smoke even when he wasn't smoking that horrible pipe. What had Teresa seen in him, anyway? He certainly made her suffer, poor thing, although she was too proud to admit it. Miss Adele had reminded her sister on each of her rare visits, usually made alone, that she could come back to the family home whenever she wanted. But Teresa had refused even to talk about it, sometimes quite rudely, despite the fact that her older sister had only wanted what was best for her, as always.

The telegram she had received from him was so worded as

to inflict maximum worry through a dearth of information. He had done it on purpose, of course. "Teresa sick STOP Wants to see you STOP Jacob." Truly, what could she conclude from that? How serious was Teresa's condition? It must be quite serious, or she would never have asked her to come in such weather. And what disease had she caught, all of a sudden? Maybe it wasn't all of a sudden. It wouldn't have surprised her a bit if Teresa had been sick for a long time living with that man, but had hesitated to tell her sister about it. As soon as Adele had gauged his character, and it had not taken her long, hadn't she warned Teresa that she wasn't safe with him, that he might even be the death of her? But Teresa, with her lack of understanding and simple, open-hearted nature, had waved that dismissively away.

She tried to call her sister on the phone, something she did very rarely and unwillingly, always horrified at the thought that he might answer. She had no desire to hear his voice, let alone talk to him. Now, of course, she must steel herself to endure that unpleasantness—but the long-distance lines were down. Even when the weather was fine it was hard to make long-distance calls. The blizzard must have brought down the lines somewhere. It was a wonder she had received the telegram.

So she had no choice but to head for the railway station and catch the afternoon train. She might have called Information first to see if there were any delays, but in the turmoil that overcame her that never crossed her mind. She quickly packed some warm clothes in a small suitcase, then put a full hot water bottle on top of them as final protection in case the train got stuck in a snow-drift. She filled a thermos with tea and, after a moment's hesitation, added a little of the rum she used to make holiday cakes. She included a box of the cookies that she usually nibbled with her tea and, as a final afterthought, put in another box.

When she arrived at the station she learned that the train was indeed late, but no one knew by exactly how long; more specific information was expected in about half an hour. The man at the window where she bought her ticket gave her a compassionate look when he heard where she was going, and suggested she take a seat in the station restaurant or in the waiting room. Miss Adele had never sat by herself in a restaurant, so she headed for the waiting room.

The corridor that led to the waiting room was full of soldiers. They stood talking in small groups or sat dozing on gray, wooden footlockers or even on the cold floor, their rifles leaning against the wall. They looked exhausted and there were patches of fresh mud on their untidy uniforms. Most of them were smoking cigarettes; a thick, bluish cloud of smoke hung motionless in the gloomy corridor. Miss Adele felt ill at ease as she made her way through them, head bowed and hand held over her mouth and nose, although no one paid any attention to her.

The waiting room was not very full. Only a calamity of the sort that had befallen her could force people to travel in such cold. Miss Adele found a seat in the corner across from a family of three sitting to the right of the entrance. The man was tall and thin, sitting stiffly, already bald though he was barely into his thirties. He had taken off his coat and placed it neatly on the bench next to him beside a rather large travel bag, but he had kept his long, blue woolen scarf around his neck. His wife seemed disproportionately small compared to him. She was wearing a pretty little gray hat the same shade as her fur coat, which she had only unbuttoned, although the waiting room was heated by a tall tile stove. Her cheeks were ruddy and her forehead was lightly beaded with sweat. Between them sat a little girl about six years old. She had inherited her mother's height, so her short legs dangled, swinging restlessly, not touching the floor. Whenever she banged the heels of her high-topped shoes together her father would look at her reproachfully but without saying a word. The little girl frequently raised her lips to her mother's ear to whisper something, and her mother would reply briefly in a low voice. From time to time she wiped her daughter's nose with a large, white handkerchief.

On the other side of the waiting room, across from the stove and next to one of the windows that gave onto the empty platforms, sat a stocky officer with a heavy mustache, curled upward and waxed at the points. His heavy overcoat and sheepskin hat were hanging from a hook on a nearby wall, and a small puddle of melting snow spread around his boots. He was engrossed in a brochure, though the weak light from outside made reading rather difficult, so that he had to hold it close to his face. On the bench nearest the stove, leaning against a small hand organ, dozed an old man of very unsavory appearance. His unshaven face was gaunt and heavily wrinkled, and everything he wore seemed old and tattered. The rim of his hat was ragged, gloves that had once been white showed fingertips in two or three places, while a crooked bow tie, a thin coat with two large, conspicuous patches and flat shoes that were certainly not suited to such snow completed his ensemble.

Miss Adele did not mind waiting very much; she was accustomed to it. She had spent most of her life waiting. In her younger days it had often made her restive, though she had been unable to say exactly what she was waiting for. In any case, whatever she was expecting had never happened, and she had long since reconciled herself to that. Now she was only saddened when she felt that all she really had left was to wait for her life to pass. Like the small woman, she did not take her coat off, though she unbuttoned it. She sat with her hands folded on the muff in her lap, staring blankly out the window.

Although it was only mid-afternoon, it had already begun to grow dark. The wind had died down temporarily, allowing the big, fluffy snowflakes to fall straight down as if in dreamy slow motion, and so thickly that buildings on the other side of the platform were barely visible. The silence of the gloomy waiting room was broken infrequently: somewhere outside could be heard the distant, rhythmic banging of a hammer, and from the corridor echoed the muffled laughter of several soldiers. The little girl continued to bang her heels together from time to time despite her father's obvious displeasure. In the tile stove the large logs emitted occasional sharp crackles.

Miss Adele started out of her reverie when she heard the hand organ. Staring out the window, she had not noticed when the ragged old man woke and picked up his instrument. She had never liked music—it was always too loud for her. She had a radio at home, but even on those rare occasions when she listened to it, she always kept the sound low. She glanced angrily at the organ-grinder. Such people should be excluded from waiting rooms, she thought—or at least they should be ordered not to bother decent people with their noisy instruments. She turned, expecting to see similar views expressed on the faces of the other occupants, but all remained strangely indifferent, paying no attention to the musician.

Then Miss Adele experienced her first vision. She had just directed another angry look at the organ-grinder when, although she could still hear him playing, he disappeared—suddenly, and without warning, along with everything else that had been within her field of vision a moment before. Something else appeared instead. The waiting room was still there, but on the edges, like some sort of frame, as if a smaller picture had been placed over a larger one.

The smaller picture showed a room principally occupied by a large, brass bedstead. It looked familiar to Miss Adele, but in her initial confusion she was not able to place it, nor did she recognize the woman lying motionless in the bed, with the eyelids closed on her pale, drawn face, and hands crossed on her chest. She only realized what she was looking at when the taller of the two men sitting beside the bed raised his head and turned his watery eyes briefly in her direction. He then turned back toward the priest on the other chair, who was absorbed in reading a prayer aloud from his breviary, and said something to him she could not hear.

Miss Adele gasped in pain and raised her hands to her mouth. Her muff slipped off her lap. Her whole body shook, and her head was spinning. Only after several long moments of great effort was she able to regain partial control of herself. This certainly cannot be true, she tried to convince herself. Teresa could not be dead, if only because Jacob, with his malicious, hateful nature, would not for a moment have hesitated to inform her, taking pleasure in the suffering that the news would cause. His telegram had only said her sister was sick. It didn't even say seriously—simply, sick.

This was only a silly apparition, she thought, although very convincing, and that terrible organ-grinder was to blame. He had completely addled her brain with his impudent and unexpected music. Really, how dared he? It was only then that she realized she could see him again. He was no longer concealed by a ghostly picture. He had stopped turning the handle of his dilapidated organ, and was watching her from the other end of the waiting room. Four other pairs of eyes were looking askance at her too.

Her gasp must have caught their attention. What must they think of her now? That she was a senile old woman living in some imaginary interior world? Or even that she was clinically insane? If they knew what had just appeared to her, their conjectures would be completely confirmed. Just look what an unseemly situation such a vagrant could bring upon a decent woman! It was because of unpleasant encounters such as this that she was so disinclined to travel, or even to go out among other people. Miss Adele bent down and picked her muff up off the floor. She shook it gently and returned it to her lap, then waited stoically for the inquisitive stares to turn away.

The silence that reigned once again did not last long. It was broken by the old man near the tile stove, though this time not with his music. He was overcome by an attack of dry, wheezy coughing that appeared to come from the very bottom of his lungs. It seemed as if he would never be able to stop; at times it even resembled a death rattle. Although she was sitting some distance away, Miss Adele nonetheless took out her lace-edged handkerchief to cover her mouth, just in case. The last thing she needed right now was to get sick, like her sister. When the organ-grinder finally caught his breath, he stood up slowly, straightened his untidy clothes, raised his bulky instrument and headed ponderously for the door. Miss Adele felt relieved when he left. She only hoped that he had gone for good.

It was already quite dark in the waiting room, but it was not clear who should turn on the light. This was finally resolved by the officer, since he could no longer read beside the window. He laid the open brochure on the bench and headed toward the switch by the door, his boots squeaking on the bare wooden floor and leaving a wet trace. The very moment light poured over the large room from two bare bulbs in the high ceiling, Miss Adele's ears were once again filled with the organ-grinder's music. She thought at first that he was playing for the soldiers in the corridor, even though the music was quite clear, as if he were still here in the waiting room. But she had no time to wonder at this curious fact for just then she experienced a second vision.

The officer was returning to his seat when he was suddenly concealed by the smaller picture. Miss Adele could still hear his sloshing footsteps on the floor, but now she saw him not in the waiting room, but in some dark, bomb-cratered landscape. He was advancing cautiously, crouched down, revolver in hand, leading a small squad of soldiers, making his way through dense fog or smoke. Noiseless flashes flared up suddenly on this grayness, forcing the soldiers to hit the ground. As they were getting up after the third explosion, the officer suddenly grabbed his neck with both hands. He stood there frozen for a moment or two, and then slowly sank to the ground. His hands fell along with his body, revealing blood pouring in torrents from a gaping wound in the middle of his throat. It soaked the upper part of his overcoat that a moment before had been hanging from a hook in the waiting room.

Miss Adele quickly covered her mouth with her handkerchief, smothering a cry of horror. Terrified by the appalling scene, she closed her eyes tightly. Her rapid heartbeat seemed to boom loud as a drum. She waited for her pulse to calm down a little before she dared to look again, shuddering, at what she feared to see. But when she opened her eyes, all that greeted her was the innocuous waiting room, now harshly lit. The officer was sitting calmly in his seat by the window, once again intent on his reading.

Although she was not in the least inclined to stare at people, and particularly not at people she didn't know, for some time she could not take her eyes off the officer's powerful neck. The vision was gone, but the image of blood pouring unquenchably from it was vivid in her memory. He must have been hit by a stray bullet or shrapnel fragment. The wound seemed serious, so he had certainly lost a lot of blood before anyone could help him. How awful! thought Miss Adele. He was still relatively young. It was extremely unfair to die like that. She had to warn him of what awaited him. Then maybe he could avoid such a fate.

But she didn't do anything. She sat in her seat and finally, with great effort, lowered her eyes to her hands in her lap. What could she tell him, anyway? That she had seen a vision? That she had seen him die in a cratered battlefield? That it was all because of that ragged organ-grinder's music? She would only get tangled up in her attempts to explain something to him that she herself did not understand. He would think her an old fool, bothering people with her prattle. And what if the vision were wrong, just like the one of Teresa on her deathbed? She would look ridiculous! It was all so unpleasant. What had she done to deserve this, in addition to all her other troubles?

Somewhere from the distance came the drawn-out whistle of a locomotive. Miss Adele turned hopeful eyes to the windows. The sooner the train arrived, the sooner her suffering here would end. She expected the public-address system, located conspicuously above the door of the waiting room, to announce the train's arrival in the station, but it remained silent. Several minutes later a seemingly endless string of cars began to pass slowly by one of the platforms, a black clattering stream sliding through the barely paler night. From its lack of lighted windows, Miss Adele concluded that it must be a freight train, not scheduled to stop at the station. But if this train had arrived, that meant the track was passable.

The little girl sitting between her parents whispered something to her mother again. She nodded, and the two of them got up and headed out of the waiting room, holding hands. The father continued to sit there stiffly, staring straight ahead, paying them no attention. The moment the door closed behind the mother and daughter, the organ-grinder announced a new vision. Once again, he played so loudly and clearly that Miss Adele suddenly looked in suspicion at the two men sitting there, seemingly deaf to this obtrusive music, before she returned her fearful attention to the ominous, smaller picture, unconsciously clutching her handkerchief.

The inside of the car was cramped, particularly the back seat where the little girl was sitting. She seemed somewhat older, by maybe two or three years. She was surrounded by piles of luggage and even had a small suitcase in her lap. Father was driving and he often turned his head to say something to Mother on the seat next to him. Although she couldn't hear him, Miss Adele concluded by his wife's demeanor that he must be reprimanding her. Her head was bowed, and she frequently raised her fingers to wipe away tears.

Everything happened very quickly: the lights of another car suddenly appeared around a curve, aimed straight at them; Mother opened her mouth in a silent cry, her eyes staring; Daughter instinctively lifted the suitcase to shield herself; Father wrenched the steering wheel to avoid the collision, but was unable to turn it back again in time. The car flew off the road and started to plunge down a steep hillside, rolling over and over. Seen from inside, the car seemed to be immobile while the whole world spun madly around it. And then there was a violent crash against a boulder at the bottom of the cliff and flames that suddenly engulfed the whole of the smaller picture.

This time Miss Adele did not even try to hold back her cry. She jumped up from her seat, holding her muff to prevent it falling to the floor again. The fiery image suddenly melted before her when she changed position, to be replaced by two bewildered faces. But now they made no difference—no more misgivings about inappropriate behaviour could stop her.

What had happened to the officer was horrifying, but his death had at least been something one could expect, a professional risk run in the line of duty, while this was a true tragedy. An entire family—and the child in particular! She had only begun to live, so to speak. No, this could not be allowed. Even if she looked ridiculous and they thought she was a crazy old fool, the child must be saved. Adele had to tell Father about this fateful event. All at once she felt certain that it would take place, that all the visions she had seen would come to pass. This, of course, meant that the vision about Teresa must also be a true one, but right then the inexorability of that event seemed less important to her.

She walked over to the man with the blue scarf and got straight to the point. "You must drive carefully, sir. You mustn't argue with your wife. Because another car will appear and then..."

She did not have time to tell him what would happen. The loudspeaker suddenly crackled and a mechanical female voice announced the arrival of the long-awaited passenger train. The door to the waiting room opened at the same instant and Mother and Daughter returned. Behind them came the sounds of the soldiers' commotion in the corridor. The woman looked at her husband inquisitively as she came up to him, but he only shrugged. The officer rushed past them, trying to put on his overcoat with one hand while holding his sheepskin hat and brochure in the other.

Miss Adele knew that she had to go on, that what she had said was insufficient and confused. She could tell by his expression that he hadn't understood a thing and didn't believe her. But somehow she couldn't find the right words. A feeling of increasing helplessness came over her as the precious seconds passed, and with them the chance to do something. Instead she just stood there, mute and foolishly staring. Finally, Father ran out of patience. He picked up his coat and travel bag from the bench and led his wife and daughter toward the exit.

Miss Adele was left alone in the waiting room, feeling useless and discomfited. She had not succeeded in warning them, and had made a fool of herself by trying. If she tried to approach them again on the train, they would certainly refuse to listen to her. Yet she had to do something—she couldn't give up on a literal matter of life and death. But in her overwhelming panic she could think of nothing. She heard the rhythmic clacking of metal wheels outside, and soon the nearest platform was filled with a moving string of lighted windows. That snapped Miss Adele out of her paralysis. She would think of something later, now she had to hurry. Since the train was late it would certainly not stay in the station very long.

She picked up her suitcase and hurried toward the corridor. The soldiers were no longer scattered but had assembled into two columns, ready to move out, the officer to the fore, giving sharp orders. Just as Miss Adele was heading past the military formation toward the platform, the organ-grinder's music started to blare all around her. At first she thought the ragged old man had somehow reached the public-address system and was now seeking to cheer the entire station with his unbearable music through all the loudspeakers. It was so loud that she wished she had both hands free, so she could cover her ears. But that desire soon lost urgency in the face of another vision.

She could not see the context; there was nothing but a pile of bodies. They covered the entire smaller picture, in which nothing moved: these were the corpses of the young soldiers she now heard marching in the background. Death had visited them in countless horrific forms. Here the back of a head was blown off, there was a bloody hole instead of an eye; scattered intestines, a red crater across a chest, stumps where there used to be legs, torsos without heads, unrecognizable joints of human flesh... some battlefield's insane harvest of youth curtailed and beauty mutilated.

Miss Adele started to trip over her feet and lose her balance. The last of the marching soldiers turned toward her briefly but had no chance to offer help. Their commanding officer was in a hurry to see his detachment settled on the train to military glory. She was overcome by nausea. Her hand over her mouth, leaning against the wall, she staggered down the corridor and found herself in the station's main hall. She headed for the restroom, not the platform, but ran into two waves of arriving passengers heading for the exit. In other circumstances this would have embarrassed her exceedingly, but now she barely even noticed.

Miss Adele spent a long time leaning over the toilet bowl, until her stomach was completely empty. Although it had been very disagreeable, vomiting had brought her some relief. She splashed her pale face with icy water from the sink, then wiped it with her lace-edged handkerchief, neglecting to remove the drops that had been sprinkled on the upper part of her coat. When she finally returned to the station hall, it was empty. The train was long gone, bearing into the snowy night people about whom she knew what she would have given anything not to know.

When she went back to the window to get a refund on her ticket, the ticket-seller had no way of understanding the sudden sigh that escaped from her as she watched him work, nor the bewilderment that appeared in her eyes, as if they were looking at something terrible, and not these commonplace surroundings. He was even less able to hear the repetitious music of the organ-grinder ringing in her ears—unsurprisingly, since there was no organ-grinder nearby.

The taxi driver who picked her up from the station was equally confused. Looking at her for a moment in his rear-view mirror, he saw her hold her hands over her ears and shake her head, eyes tightly closed. He was used to passengers acting oddly at times, but they were usually young people, not serious-looking, elderly women. He thought of asking her if she needed help, but abandoned the idea. He was suddenly sure he could do nothing to help this lady.

Back home, Miss Adele found a new telegram on the mat below the front door. She locked it away unread with the previous telegram in the carved wooden box where she kept her photo album and old letters. There was no need to open it, since she knew what it said. Just as she knew she would not go to Teresa's funeral. Not because the trip would be too strenuous, nor because she could not tolerate Jacob, but because she would inevitably encounter people along the way. And that had already become a nightmare she could hardly endure.

She had not been one to go out much before, and now she scarcely left the house. This did not seem unusual to any of her neighbors, since she was known to be a woman of retiring character who was not on intimate terms with anyone. Her behavior had become rather strange, indeed, whenever she ran into anyone, but it is well known that old maids sometimes lose their marbles.

Miss Adele's final wait took its time. She would have found it easier to bear could she have seen the end, but the organ-grinder who played for everyone else refused to play for her. After pondering this at length, she could not tell whether he was being especially kind to her or whether this was his ultimate damnation.

the puzzle

5

Mr. Adam only started to paint late in life, after his retirement. It happened quite unexpectedly. For the first sixty-five years of his life he had never shown any predisposition toward painting, for which he had neither talent nor interest. The arts in general attracted him very little.

The only exception might have been music, though he didn't really enjoy it. Sometimes he would find a radio station devoted mainly to music and leave it on low, just enough to dispel the silence that surrounded him during his long, dreary hours at work. It didn't matter what sort of music was being played; almost any would serve his purpose equally well, although he preferred instrumentals since singing distracted him. All he did at home was sleep, and often not even that, so there was little opportunity for anything else.

Retirement brought Mr. Adam an abundance of empty

hours which he must fill. Experience gained at work had taught him that whenever he had to wait an indeterminate time for something, he had to impose obligations upon himself, and then discharge them doggedly, regardless of how unusual they might seem. This at least gave a semblance of meaning to everything. And one could not live without some meaning, however illusory.

He set himself one obligation for every day of the week. On Sunday he cooked, something he had never done before. He bought the biggest cookbook he could find in the bookstore and set himself to prepare every dish in it, in alphabetical order. The uncertainty of how far he dared hope to get at this tempo did not disturb him. He was aware that he would require extreme longevity to reach the end of the book, but that was of no importance to him.

He followed the instructions for each recipe to the letter, and the only trouble he encountered was when they were not specific enough, but allowed the cook to use his own judgement or taste. He did not like everything he cooked, but that did not bother him greatly. He ate his culinary creations down to the last spoonful, throwing nothing away. This was almost a matter of honor to him. Sometimes, when the recipe was intended for several people, he ate the same food the whole week through.

On Monday Mr. Adam rode his bicycle. This was also a new departure. He learned how to ride easily and quite rapidly, despite his advanced age. He was not deterred by bad weather, though he would dress accordingly. The only trouble he had was when the rain spattered his glasses, unpleasantly fogging his vision. He preferred to ride without glasses in a downpour, though that rendered his vision equally foggy.

He always took the same route, each time increasing the distance a little. He tried to conserve his energy so he had enough left to go back by bike. He was only forced to return by other means of transport on the few occasions when there was a sudden turn in the weather, or he was overcome by fatigue. His conscience always plagued him when he gave up like that.

Unlike cooking, cycling had its limits. The route he took never actually ended, since it connected to many others, but even if he were to ride the whole day without stopping, which was not very likely, at midnight he would be required to stop. Tuesday was not for bike riding, but imposed its own obligation.

While still employed, he had read very little except professional journals. Not because there was no opportunity—many of his colleagues read for pleasure to pass the time at work—but because it seemed to him a sign of insufficient dedication to the job. Of course, his work would not have suffered for it, particularly since computers had taken over the bulk of his responsibilities. Now he decided to make up at least partially for this lapse. He became a member of the town library and went there every Tuesday. He entered as soon as it opened and stayed until it closed, only taking a short break early in the afternoon to eat something.

His initial subject was science fiction. This was a natural choice, but Mr. Adam soon gave it up. What he read about first contact seemed unsophisticated for the most part, often to the point of inanity—pulled out of thin air, at best. The number of writers demonstrating any knowledge of the real state of things was quite small, though such knowledge was easy enough to obtain. Disappointed, he was briefly tempted to abandon reading entirely. But giving up in the face of adversity was not in his nature, and besides, he had paid his dues a year in advance. Finally, were he to stop going to the library he would have to think up a new obligation for Tuesday, and that prospect did not please him at all.

He found a solution to this problem, using the same means he had often resorted to at work. Whenever his search in one area drew a blank, he simply broadened his field of vision. Not knowing what else to choose, this time he broadened the field to the farthest limit, like suddenly taking in the whole sky instead of one small sector. Instead of science fiction he chose literature in its entirety, but as this turned out to be far greater even than the cookbook, he had no idea at first where to begin.

The main catalog was indexed by author, and he briefly considered adhering to that order. But then he thought again, and concluded this would not be a satisfactory approach. He spent some time at the library computer, classifying titles by publication date, and finally obtained a list of books from the oldest to the most recent. The scale of this list did not discourage him at all—he had become accustomed to such challenges long ago. He started to read steadily, without rushing, as if all the time in the world lay before him.

On Wednesdays Mr. Adam went to the zoo. The middle of the week was the right time to visit, when there were far fewer visitors than during weekends. Moreover, if the weather was bad, he would often see no one in the vicinity for long periods. That suited him best. Ideally he would have liked to be completely alone at the zoo, but of course, he was never able to count on that.

Mr. Adam did not behave like the ordinary sort of visitor, who just wanders around enjoying himself. First he found out which animals were housed in the zoo, then he drew up a schedule of visits. Each animal was allotted a whole day. Few of the zoo's inhabitants were worthy of such dedication, but the systematic patience with which Mr. Adam approached everything did not allow him to act otherwise.

He would arrive in the morning at the chosen cage and sit in front of it. When there was no bench he brought a small folding chair from home. He would stay in that spot until nightfall, doing nothing but observe the animal carefully through the bars. He did not know exactly what to expect. Certainly nothing special. What he hoped for was at least a certain reaction to his presence, just an awareness that he was there, perhaps a glance that deliberately crossed his own. Anything short of complete disregard.

It was actually quite easy to attract the animals' attention by offering them food, but Mr. Adam never did. It would be a form of cheating, and he would brook no cheating. Therefore he took no food with him, not even for himself. When he left the zoo on a Wednesday evening, he was often faint with hunger.

On Thursdays Mr. Adam visited churches. Not being religious, he had never been to such places before, and was surprised to learn that the town held sixteen of them. Sometimes he had to walk the whole day in order to take them all in. He could have used public transport, of course, which would have sped things up considerably, but that would have run contrary to Mr. Adam's basic intention. His Monday bike ride was by no means sufficient to keep him in shape, and his need for additional exercise was the more acute after spending all Wednesday sitting still at the zoo. What could be more appropriate than a seriously long walk?

In order to avoid the tedium of repeating the same walk every time, Mr. Adam took a different route every Thursday. This was not done at random; he had worked out a precise plan. He approached it as a simple problem in combinatorial mathematics. There were far more ways of ordering the sixteen points than he imagined he would ever need. The itineraries greatly varied in length, because the algorithm he had chosen took no account of the distance between the churches. He bore up stoically under this inconsiderate mathematical dictate, consoling himself with the reflection that he found longer walks more enjoyable.

Mr. Adam could have visited points other than churches. In principle, the direction of his walks was immaterial to him, so he could not have explained why he had made churches his choice. Luckily, no one ever asked him, which saved him from embarrassment. On reaching a church he began by walking all the way around it, examining it inquisitively, as if seeing it for the first time. Then he would take a little rest, sitting in the churchyard if there was one, before continuing on his way.

In time he got to know the exteriors of all sixteen churches quite well, and came to regard himself as a real expert in this field. He believed that he alone had noted some of the details. For example, there was always an even number of birds' nests under the eaves. Who knows why? He rarely felt any urge to examine the churches' interiors. He was only tempted to enter on two or three occasions, but he always refrained, and here again he was unable to say what it was that had dissuaded him.

Friday was his day to go to the movies. Mr. Adam would always watch four films in a row, from mid-afternoon to late in the evening. This was by any standard too much. After the second film his impressions were already becoming confused, and by the end of the fourth he would feel truly exhausted, as though he had been working at some strenuous task rather than sitting in a comfortable seat the whole time. But this did not prompt him to decrease the number of films.

Mr. Adam was not the least bit selective regarding the repertoire. He did not have a favorite film genre, although he felt most relaxed watching romantic comedies. Action films left him rather indifferent, and though they were loud as a rule, he even managed to doze off during them, particularly if they were the last of that day's four. He found thrillers unconvincing, though not as much as most science fiction films. Those sometimes appeared outrageously idiotic; he could never understand why filmgoers got so excited about them. Overly erotic scenes embarrassed him, but fortunately that was not noticeable in the dark.

Although it might have appeared that Mr. Adam chose his films at random, this was not at all the case. He bought his tickets with great care, concentrating on films that were expected to sell out. Just before the lights dimmed, Mr. Adam would stand up for a moment and look all around. He would feel annoyed should he spot any empty seats. Those empty places would bother him until the end of the show. He only felt at ease in a full house. That alone could temporarily lighten the burden of solitude which, like some sinister inheritance, hung over from his former work.

Mr. Adam passed Saturdays in the park. He needed to spend time outside in the fresh air after so many hours indoors the previous day. Late in the morning he would go to the large city park with its pond in the middle, and head for the bench where he always sat. On the rare occasions when someone was already sitting in the place he considered his own, on the far left-hand end of the bench next to the wrought iron armrest, Mr. Adam would wait unobtrusively to one side for the bench to come free. It did not bother him if the remainder of the bench was occupied, though he avoided entering into conversation with strangers.

On warm, sunny days he would stay there until dusk, doing nothing but idly watching what was happening around him: people strolling by, dogs chasing each other frantically on the grass, leaves rustling in the surrounding treetops, birds gliding silently through the blue sky, sudden ripples on the smooth surface of the pond. Until recently this idleness would have seemed an extremely foolish waste of time. Now, however, the tables were turned. He saw everything which had gone before as a waste of time. All his previous life. All the years, all the effort, all the hopes.

That was not how it had seemed, at any rate not in the beginning. Not in the least. It was a pioneering time of great excitement. Great expectations—and great naiveté. They thought that contact was only a matter of time. The cosmos was teeming with life, messages were streaming between worlds, all that was needed was to prick up our electronic ears to hear them. Without this optimistic certainty the money for the first projects would never have been found—investments that could pay off stupendously as soon as the inexhaustible wealth of knowledge started to pour in from the stars.

Mr. Adam had fond memories of those early days, despite later disappointments. There was something romantic in the anticipation that overcame him whenever he put on his earphones. He spent countless hours listening to the cacophony streaming from the skies, straining to recognize some sort of orderly system in it. Like all his colleagues, he secretly hoped that he would be the first to hear the signal.

But as time passed and nothing arrived except inarticulate noise, the true proportions of the task started to emerge. Since listening to the closest star systems produced no results, there was a shift to more distant ones, but each new step brought a substantial increase in their number. The initial enthusiasm foundered when it was established that more than one generation might be needed to complete the task. This led many people to leave the search for extraterrestrial life in favor of more promising areas, and financiers were less and less willing to continue investing in something so vague and unreliable.

Fortunately, at that point computers were introduced, with their numerous advantages over people: they are incomparably faster, more effective and dependable, and do not quickly lose heart in the face of failure. Even so, Mr. Adam did not look upon their use with total approval. Computers reduced people to commonplace assistants whose sole purpose was to serve them. What had begun as a noble project for the chosen few degenerated into a routine technical duty that almost anyone could perform—mere waiting, leached of any true excitement. The last remnants of romance vanished without a trace.

After several decades had passed and the computers had meticulously checked many millions of star systems but detected no sign of extraterrestrial intelligence, Mr. Adam felt a certain gloomy exultation. His feelings were paradoxical, because only under opposite circumstances, with contact made, would he be able to say that his life's work had meaning. On the other hand, contact achieved with the assistance of computers would to him be some sort of injustice, almost an anticlimax.

Despite the silence of the cosmos, the search programs were not discontinued. Although large, the number of investigated stars was trifling compared to the total number of suns in the galaxy. In principle, one of the giant radio telescopes could start receiving the long-awaited message from the very next spot in the sky. However, as his retirement approached, Mr. Adam became more and more skeptical in this regard.

It was not just the realization that the prospects of finding Others within his lifetime were negligible; he could somehow reconcile himself to that if he was sure they were on the right track. But the suspicion started to trouble him that the reason for failure lay not in the fact that only a tiny part of the sky had been investigated, but rather in something much more fundamental. What if some of the basic assumptions upon which the entire project was founded were wrong?

Maybe there was no one out there after all. Maybe sentient beings were so unlikely that they had only appeared in one place. Everyone was convinced of the opposite, but this conviction had no solid basis. Behind it might lie an unwillingness to accept the terrifying fact of cosmic solitude. As the years passed, Mr. Adam started to feel anxious under the unbounded wasteland. The starry sky pressed heavily upon him at times. The strange need arose for some sort of shelter, for consolation.

Suppose extraterrestrials exist and are communicating, but we don't recognize it? What if they were doing it in some other way, and not the way we presumed? Mr. Adam had never asked himself this question seriously. Whenever it stole quietly into his consciousness he would expel it hurriedly, with a sense of hostility and guilt, as any true believer rejects a heretical thought. All his sober, scientific being opposed it. Similar inconsistencies had prevented him from coming to like science fiction.

He still considered this the proper approach, despite all the unfulfilled hopes in the life that yawned behind him. And at the end of the day, what other means besides electromagnetic waves could be used to communicate between the stars? With regard to his past, the daily obligations he set himself helped put it out of his mind. Perhaps these obligations really were meaningless, but the problem of meaning no longer plagued him. He enjoyed everything he was doing now, even idling in the park each Saturday, and that pleasure was all that mattered. In any case, he was not just idly passing the time. He had recently started to paint.

Music had been the catalyst. Upon reaching the park one

Saturday at the beginning of summer, he found a bandstand had been erected near his bench. It had not been there seven days previously, nor had anything heralded its advent. This had irritated Mr. Adam to no end. Although pretty, with its slender columns and domed roof, he considered it an unconscionable desecration of the environment. In addition, the bandstand largely blocked his view of the pond, and he seriously considered looking for another place to sit. But habit won out and he stayed on his bench, scornfully endeavoring to disregard the interloper.

This ceased to be possible when musicians climbed onto the bandstand at noon. They were formally dressed and the conductor even wore a tuxedo with a large white flower in his lapel. They sat on chairs placed in a circle and spent some time tuning their instruments. Mr. Adam found this dissonance an additional nuisance. It not only sounded awful but started to attract park visitors, and a rather large crowd soon formed. A crowd of people, however, was the last thing Mr. Adam wanted after his Friday spent in a packed movie theater.

He would have to move after all. He couldn't stand this. But just as he started to rise the music began. He stopped halfway, transfixed, then slowly sat down again on the bench. All at once he was no longer surrounded by too many people, his bad mood disappeared, and nothing existed beyond the music. He stared fixedly at the bandstand, immobile, listening intently.

This paralysis did not last long. He came out of it suddenly and began feverishly rummaging through his jacket pockets. It seemed to take forever to find what he was after. He always carried a notebook and pen with him. Since retirement he had not written anything in it, but he carried it with him nonetheless. He opened it hurriedly and started to draw. He dared not miss a thing.

He drew short, brusque lines, just like a stenographer taking rapid dictation. The pages in the notebook were small, so he filled them quickly. He was afraid he would run out of pages before the music ended, but fortunately the notebook was thick enough. Even so, he made the last drawing on the brown cardboard covers. Had the music lasted a moment longer, there would not have been enough room. The very thought suddenly filled him with horror.

The listeners' echoing applause after the last chords had the effect of an alarm clock suddenly going off. Mr. Adam jerked like one waking from restless sleep; he turned this way and that in confusion for several moments as if trying to figure out where he was. He feared he would arouse the suspicion of those around him, but no one had paid any attention to the old man on the end of the bench, engrossed in his writing. All eyes were turned toward the conductor who was bowing theatrically.

Mr. Adam stood up and walked away unobtrusively. There was no reason to stay there any longer. During his extensive walks between churches he had come to know the town quite well, so he knew exactly where to find a shop with painting supplies. There might have been one closer, but he would waste more time inquiring after and finding it than it took to reach the other. The salesman noted with a smile that he was clearly preparing a serious project, judging by the quantity of materials he had purchased. Mr. Adam returned the smile, mumbled something vague, then hurried home.

Unskilled at painting, he had trouble setting up the easel properly, but then got down to work. He opened the notebook and began carefully transferring onto the canvas what he had written, as if neatly copying over rough notes taken in a hurry. He worked slowly but with passion, unaware of the passage of time. When he had finished it was already quite dark.

He did not know what he had painted. Viewed from up close it looked just like random strokes of paint. He was convinced, however, that not a single stroke of the brush had been accidental, that everything was exactly as the music ordered, in spite of his inexperience. When he moved back from the painting a bit, he thought he could make out part of a larger shape, but he wasn't sure. It suddenly crossed his mind that before him was just one piece of some larger puzzle. He thought briefly about what to do with the canvas, and then he hung it unframed on one of the bare walls.

The next Saturday he went to the park well prepared. He no longer needed the notebook as intermediary. He sat at his usual place on the bench and set up the easel in front of him, holding paintbrush and palette. In different circumstances he would have abhorred the inquisitive peering of bystanders, although a painter at work was certainly not unusual in the park. Now, however, he paid no attention, concentrating exclusively on the impending concert.

This time he painted rapidly. It lasted just as long as the music. When the applause resounded, Mr. Adam, panting and sweaty, had just finished covering the last white space with paint. Before the crowd dispersed, several pairs of eyes glanced at the painting, perplexed, since it did not depict anything recognizable. A short, elderly woman dressed in a bright orange dress stopped by the bench for a moment. She took an enormous pair of glasses out of her handbag and examined first the painting and then the painter. "Very nice," she said with a smile. She put her glasses back in her handbag, nodded in brief approval and walked away.

As a man unaccustomed to compliments, Mr. Adam felt ill at ease. The woman's words were by no means unpleasant, quite the contrary, yet he was still glad she had not lingered. He would have been in the awkward situation of having to say something in reply. He waited a while for the elderly woman to move on, then collected his equipment and hurried home. He could have stayed in the park longer—his work was completed and the day was very fine—but curiosity got the better of him.

He put the new canvas next to the other one on the wall. He had no expectations and thus was not very disappointed when it turned out they had no points in common. For a moment, though, he thought he could make out some part of a greater whole in the second painting, too, but here again it was most likely just his imagination. In the absence of any recognizable form he thought he saw something that was not actually there. This was a trap he had learned to avoid back in the early period, before computers, while listening to the stars with his own ears. If you're expecting a horseman you have to be very careful not to mistake your heartbeat for the beat of a horse's hoofs.

The next fourteen Saturdays, all summer long, each time Mr. Adam returned from the park he had one more painting to place on the wall next to the others. In time his brisk, almost frenetic painting became something of an attraction at the park, and a good many music-lovers would stand around to watch him work. He paid no attention to them. At the end of the music and painting he would quickly glance through those gathered around him, but never once did he catch sight of the slight figure in orange.

When Mr. Adam reached the park on the first Saturday in September, carrying his painting materials as usual, a surprise awaited him. The bandstand had disappeared as unexpectedly as it had arrived. It had been removed very carefully, leaving no trace behind—not even trampled grass. He darted in bewilderment around the spot where the little structure had stood, overcome by completely opposite feelings from those which had assailed him in the beginning. Now he missed the bandstand, and the environment seemed somehow naked and incomplete without it. For a moment he considered inquiring as to why it was no longer there, maybe even lodging a complaint, but he did not know where this should be done and in the end dropped the idea.

He returned home in a dejected mood and sat in the armchair facing the wall covered with paintings. The canvases formed a large square: four paintings in each of four rows. He stayed there for seven full days, only leaving the armchair to take a quick bite or go to the bathroom. He even slept there in his clothes, but the brief, restless, erratic sleep did not refresh him. He changed the distribution of the paintings from time to time. During that long week filled with almost constant pouring rain, he tried all possible combinations of the sixteen canvases.

On the evening of the following Saturday he got up from the armchair, stretched, and went to the window. Rays from the low sun in the western sky were cutting a path through patchy clouds, just like gleaming swords. He stayed there a while looking absently at the flickering play of light. Then he went to the wall and took down the paintings. He couldn't carry them all at once and had to make two trips to the basement, where he left them.

When he came up from the basement the second time, he went into the kitchen, took the large cookbook down from the shelf, opened it at the bookmark and became immersed in reading the recipe that was next in line. The following day was Sunday, his cooking day.

the violinist

6

The professor knew he would not survive the night.

Dr. Dean did not tell him that, of course. At least not to his face. But his body language confirmed the inevitable.

As usual, the doctor dropped by to see him at 11:10 in the evening, after his shift was over. Before he entered the room he spent a few minutes in the glass cubicle outside, talking quietly with the duty nurse, Mrs. Roszel. They talked in low voices, periodically looking through the glass at the sick man's bed. At one point Mrs. Roszel shook her bowed head and raised clenched fingers to her eyes, as if to wipe away tears.

When he appeared before the professor, Dr. Dean tried his best to appear relaxed and cheerful, but he was not a very good actor. He must have had to play the role of false optimist many times in his long career, but the small things still gave him away. He avoided looking the professor in the eye, finding various excuses to turn his glance aside. He checked his pulse, though they both knew it served no purpose. Then he tightened and smoothed the bedclothes with brusque, nervous movements, which was also unnecessary and in any case Mrs. Roszel's job, which she performed frequently and expertly.

Then he went to stand by the large window and stare out at the spring Princeton night. Gusts of rain beat against the pane, making ephemeral streaks that distorted the doctor's dimly reflected face. He sighed, and told his patient that he actually envied him. What he wouldn't give to be in his place! The professor was already in bed, but before the doctor lay a good half-hour's drive through this foul weather, to be followed by at least another hour filled with various obligations, all to be discharged before he could finally go to bed himself. But such was life. Some people were lucky and some were not.

He hesitated after saying this, because the conclusion was somehow inappropriate, given the circumstances. His intention had been to cheer the professor up and instill some hope, however unfounded, but it seemed he had inadvertently gone too far. It might have appeared cynical or even cruel to claim that someone whose hours were literally numbered was lucky. He turned from the window, and for the first time looked at his patient's haggard face.

The expression on it made the doctor feel foolish, for it told him that his acting had been as unsuitable as it was inept. He had seen that expression before, albeit rarely. The professor was

118

not only conscious of what awaited him, but prepared for it. He did not expect any consolation, nor did he need it. This was no place for empty words.

The doctor went up to the bed and shook the old man's cold, slender hand. "Good night, Professor." It took considerable effort to keep his voice from trembling.

"Goodbye, Doctor."

Dr. Dean gently patted the back of his patient's hand with his free one. He tried to smile, but only managed a grimace. Then he turned and, more hastily than he liked or had intended, left the patient's room. As he put on his raincoat and hat in the cubicle, he exchanged a few more words with Mrs. Roszel.

Ten minutes later the nurse went into the patient's room to prepare him for the night. She began by giving him an oval blue pill. The Professor was given one every night before sleeping, and he would try to swallow it quickly with a little water because it tasted bitter. He took it as dutifully as ever, though he felt it was a pointless exercise. Not to have done so might have been awkward for Mrs. Roszel, and she took care of him not only conscientiously but with affection.

As she needlessly straightened his bedclothes, she murmured something about the rain that had been pouring ceaselessly since early afternoon. Then she went to the window and closed the curtains. The drumming of the heavy drops became suddenly muffled and distant. She went back to the bed and spent a few moments silently arranging the yellow wildflowers on his night table. It seemed as if she wanted to say something else, but was hesitating for some reason. When she left the room finally, still without saying it, the professor felt relieved. He did not feel like talking to Mrs. Roszel right then.

The nurse stopped at the entrance to her cubicle and turned off the strip light. "I'll be here if you need anything, Professor," she said softly. "Just call for me. Good night."

"Good night, Mrs. Roszel."

He looked at her through the glass, sitting at her small desk. Now the only source of light in both rooms was a lamp with a thick yellow shade. Its dull glow made the white ribbon that kept the nurse's hair off her forehead look like a golden aureole. She had lowered her head to read a book without taking her usual last glance at her patient.

The pill soon began to take effect. He first felt the dull, unremitting pain in his stomach soften to barely noticeable discomfort, as if a large pillow had been placed over his abdomen. Then the familiar feeling of floating began. Suddenly the bed seemed to disappear and he was lying in empty space, completely weightless. He knew it was only an illusion, but that did nothing to lessen the intoxicating pleasure of the feeling. Not even tonight.

The floating would not last long. Before he fell asleep he would experience a brief feeling that his body had separated into an assembly of weakly connected spheres. Soundlessly, the fragile links between them would start to dissolve, and he would melt into nothingness, merging with the black infinity that surrounded him. His last conscious thought would be that this must be what dying was like. Courtesy of the blue pill, he had died every night since his arrival at the hospital.

Come morning he would wake in a bad mood. It bothered him that he was not afraid of dying. Death seemed somehow attractive; it was almost as if he wanted to die, and he felt that he should not feel like that. If for no other reason, he hoped he would not die before finding the answers to several questions that had plagued him throughout his adult life. It would be quite unjust if he were denied them—but perhaps the world was only orderly, and not just. Certainly, there was very little time left for justice to be done.

On this occasion, however, he did not break up into spheres. He was prevented by the sudden intrusion of music. It was barely audible but certainly present, though he could not determine the source; it seemed to come from all around him. Mrs. Roszel kept a small radio on her desk, but she would never play it this late. He looked in the nurse's direction. She was still engrossed in her book, apparently not hearing a thing.

A violin was weaving a slow, almost dreamy melody. He did not recognize it at once though he had played the violin since childhood, but something stirred in the depths of his memory, striving to reach the surface. For a despairing moment he thought it would fail; that the memory, like so many others, would stay bound forever below the thick webbing that enveloped his aged mind. Then the sound, as if wanting to help, grew a tiny bit louder—and a bolt of lightning flashed through the gap of sixty years, taking him back to that long-ago summer day in northern Italy.

The small town in which he found himself as he walked the back roads from Milan to Genoa seemed to be completely deserted, even here on the main square, but this did not surprise him. All small places give such an impression during the siesta hour between two and four o'clock in the afternoon, when the inhabitants retreat from the unbearable heat into the shuttered cool of their homes.

This did not bother him very much. The fewer local people he ran into, the fewer difficulties he would have. He was a shy fifteen-year-old, and he found the language difficult. Almost no one understood his native German, and he had only a very limited command of the melodious speech of this area, with its open, resonant vowels. So he took pains to enter into conversation with people only when necessary, shrinking from their presumed distaste for his accent that must sound to them like the screech of rusty gears.

The piazza was approximately square in shape, with a small fountain in the middle. The young man put his canvas rucksack on the ground and started to fill his cupped hands with water from the arching stream. He splashed his face with water, letting it drip, and then looked around, head raised, squinting at the white stone façades. His eyes, used to the monotonous grayness of northern lands, constantly ached from the bright colors of Italy. Everything around him was vibrating, twinkling, glimmering, bursting. He had the feeling of being trapped in a crystal that absorbed light from all sides, but did not let it out again.

The silence was suddenly broken by the sound of a violin. It came from the top of a wide, three-story building that was separated from a church belfry by an extremely narrow, shaded street. The window in the garret was open, probably the only one unshuttered in the whole square, and in the room behind it someone had chosen to fill this stagnant, bright, deserted hour with music. It was not a student practicing, but an experienced violinist, a master whose fingers had total command of the instrument.

The chance listener next to the fountain stared, enchanted, at the high window. Even had he not been a skilled violinist himself, there was no way he could have remained unaffected. Cascades of pure harmony streamed down from above as if from heaven. They penetrated deep inside him, to the very center of his being, where they created resonant reflections. To devote his utmost concentration to listening, he closed his eyes.

He was trying to expel the omnipresent light to take best advantage of the sound, but without success. The light did not disappear under his lowered eyelids. Not only was it still there, it suppressed everything else with the power of its unabated radiance. And then, in a moment of revelation, he understood.

The light was still there because that was what the music was all about. Could there be anything more fitting? What was invoked could not have been presented to him so comprehensively by any other means. He was inside the light, and its secrets started to peel away before him, finally displaying the wondrous simplicity of its essence.

He stayed there so long, motionless, listening to the light, that he lost track of time. Something very strange had happened to time. Its course seemed to decelerate, gradually at first, then exponentially, until it finally stopped, frozen in a timeless ray that rushed through strangely distorted space. Under the tremendous pressure of light, space started to undulate, turn and twist, until it was transformed into a vortex that carried him, powerfully and irresistibly, toward the black point deep within its center. The point became a circle, then a wide opening in the fabric of reality, then an immense pit of deepest night, sucking him into itself like a speck of dust.

When he came to his senses he was at first uncertain where he was. For a moment he thought he was still in the heart of darkness, but then he realized it was not total, for it was pierced by sunbeams that slanted like sparkling spears through narrow windows in a thick stone wall. The rays were multicolored because of the stained glass they had passed through. The music had ceased.

The young man realized he was lying on something cold and hard. He tried to get up, but a pair of hands appeared and gently but firmly pushed him back. A figure in a brown mantle bent over him; it was a priest, with graying hair and beard, wearing small, round, wire-rimmed glasses. He smiled at the young man and began to speak. The young man could make out only a few words in the deluge of Italian: sun, fall, brought into the church.

He started to get up again, hastily explaining to the priest that he had to return to the square as soon as possible so as to hear the remainder of the music of light—it meant so much to him. Otherwise he was fine, there was no need to worry: he had experienced enlightenment, not sunstroke. The priest's only reply was an uncomprehending shrug, but this time there was no need for the priest's hands to stop him from getting up. He had not even reached a sitting position when his head started to swim. Overcome by exhaustion, he lay back down on the marble platform by the wall of the church on which they had placed him.

The priest reached for the wet cloth on the weary traveler's forehead and started to wipe it over his cheeks and neck. He was still talking, but the young man could make even less sense of it than before. He stopped listening, as despair filled his soul. If only he had stayed there a little longer! If only that vortex hadn't whisked him away so soon, he could have grasped the essence of light. As it was, he could only remember broken fragments, loose threads from the tapestry, pebbles detached from the mosaic. But at least he knew the mosaic existed and that it was flawless in its irreducible, self-evident necessity. Yet it seemed he had no right to hope ever to see it again, though he knew that he would devote the rest of his life to its tireless pursuit.

It was sunset when he left the church. He still felt a bit light-headed, but he had to be on his way. The piazza was now full of people, and the shutters on the windows stood wide—all but one. He spent some time before the entrance to the three-story building whose highest window was now only a blind, mute eye, but in the end he did not seek out the musician in the garret. It was not his poor knowledge of Italian that prevented him, for he would have done the same thing if he could have spoken German. What could he say to the Violinist, in any language? Moreover, he suspected that He was no longer there at all.

There was no radiance this time. Here in the gloom of the hospital room, he no longer had to close his eyes to listen to the message of the music. The thrill he had experienced once, so long ago, was not here, nor would it have suited this period of his life or his present circumstances. All that he felt, aside from the intoxicating effect of the blue pill, was a moment of happi-ness coursing gently through him, stemming from the knowl-edge that there was justice in the world, after all.

The great mosaic appeared before him, woven from vibrat-ing threads of air. It was almost completely filled in. He knew perfectly well which pebbles were missing. He had not been allowed to find them himself, as he had the others, but that no longer mattered; he had long ago discarded vanity. All that mattered was to see them at last, during the short time that remained to him.

The violin began to build shapes out of sound that slotted perfectly into the empty spaces. Each part represented a distinct revelation: amazingly simple, magnificently complex, wondrously unbelievable, insanely unacceptable. Now he understood why he would never have been able to find some of the answers. He simply did not have the right questions.

When the grand architecture of tones was finally complete, he had to confront its most disturbing characteristic: the whole and its parts were not in harmony. When he focused on the whole, the parts became fuzzy—and vice versa. He could not concentrate his internal eye on both at the same time. Once everything inside him would have rebelled at this imperfection, but not any longer: it was his preconceptions that had been wrong, of course. The world did not have to be orderly, at least not in the way he had imagined it. The Violinist based his composition on completely different principles.

He did not realize at first that the music had stopped. It was only when the mosaic came apart, giving way to the dark space it had temporarily occupied, that he became aware of the silence. He lay there confused for several moments, staring in front of him. Something must surely follow, this seemed inevitable. Death, perhaps? Was there any moment more suitable to die? But nothing happened. The spheres were still tightly grouped together.

At the thought of death he was overcome with fear. That had never happened before, but now something had undermined his previous readiness to die. For a while he could not identify it, but then it dawned on him: if he were to die right then, he would take the knowledge he had just gained to his grave. It would be as if nothing had happened, as if he had not finally comprehended. He had longed for it primarily to satisfy his own curiosity, but now that seemed selfish. No, he must at all costs leave a record of what he had learned.

But how? What could he do, lying here on his deathbed? And how much time did he have left? Certainly not much. He felt a cold wave of panic creep down the back of his neck. He started to look feverishly around the dark room, perceiving the outlines of familiar objects. Nothing he saw seemed of any help, until the lighted figure of the nurse in her cubicle came into his field of vision. His heart began to beat faster. That was it! There was no other choice. She was his last hope.

"Mrs. Roszel," he called, his voice raised and impatient.

The nurse lifted her eyes from her book, then got up and hurried to her patient.

As he watched her approach, it crossed his mind that he didn't actually know how to tell her what he had to say. The best thing would be if he had a violin. Then he could play it all to her, transmitting what he had just heard with utmost fidelity. There would be nothing of the vagueness, ambiguity or imperfection that went with words. Everything would be crystal clear, even the most difficult aspects. But there was no violin, unfortunately. He had to rely on language.

He did not hesitate for a moment over which language to use. The gears might sound rusty, but they fit together most precisely, leaving the least room for idle motion, friction and resistance. He thought with a smile how strange it was that this language, which came nearest to music in terms of expressiveness, was farthest away in terms of sonority. In addition, it was the language to which he felt closest. He would never have been able to express something as complex in a foreign language. Even in his mother tongue he would have considerable trouble.

There was no time to waste on an introduction so he went straight to the point as soon as Mrs. Roszel reached the head of the bed. He spoke quickly, concisely wherever possible, more extensively when that could not be avoided. He was full of sympathy for the expression of bewilderment and disbelief upon her face, and for her periodic helpless shrug of the shoulders. What he was revealing to her was the very foundation that upheld the universe. Fortunately, she did not need to try to understand what he was saying. It would be enough to remember his words, clear and coherent, so as to transmit them faithfully to those who were capable of comprehension. That, at least, would not be difficult.

He was describing the last part of the puzzle when he felt the links between the spheres finally loosen. He was not afraid that time would run out before he finished. There was justice in the world, was there not? The ways of the Violinist might be subtle, but He was certainly not malicious. What would be the sense in stopping him now, at the very end, after everything He had offered him? None, of course. The professor continued to speak softly to Mrs. Roszel, who was still listening carefully. The patient darkness waited for him to reach the end before engulfing him. He fell into it cheerfully, with a feeling of accomplishment. He had given the world his greatest legacy. Had he dared hope for anything greater?

the violin-maker

7

To the police inspector, it was an open-and-shut case. Mr. Tomasi, master violin-maker, had committed suicide by jumping from the window of the garret of the three-story building where he lived and ran his celebrated workshop. The tragic incident was reported by two eyewitnesses, a baker's roundsmen, delivering bread and rolls, who had been crossing the square early that morning. After hesitating a moment they had fearfully approached the place where the unfortunate man lay. He showed no signs of life, even though they could not see any external injuries.

Inspector Muratori quickly arrived at the scene of the incident and found out from the agitated young men, who had never seen death firsthand before, that nothing had heralded the falling body. They had heard no sounds before the dull thud on the sidewalk, which had frightened the pigeons at the little fountain in the middle of the square like a sudden detonation. Most suicides who take their lives by jumping from a height make their intentions known by shouting once they have stepped into the abyss and it is too late to change anything. Only those who are firmly convinced they are doing the right thing remain silent to the end.

One glance at the three-story building told Inspector Muratori where Mr. Tomasi had jumped from. The only open window was in the garret. Actually, he could have jumped off the roof, but there was no reason to choose such a steep, inaccessible place since the window was far more suitable and served his purpose equally well. Although one might not expect it of a suicide, the policeman knew that they did not, as a rule, make their last moments more difficult than necessary.

His examination of the inside of the house revealed nothing to conflict with the suicide hypothesis—on the contrary. When he climbed up to the garret that looked out onto the square, the inspector found the door locked from the inside. This was a precautionary measure typical of someone who did not want to be deterred from carrying out his intention. The door had to be forced, because there was no way to push the key out of the lock so as to open it with a skeleton key. The small room was sparsely furnished: a table and four chairs, a single bed, a washstand with a basin and pitcher in the corner, a large mirror. There was no rug on the floor, no curtains at the window, no pictures on the walls.

Mr. Umbertini, the tall, thin man in his late twenties who was the late master violin-maker's assistant and lived alone with him in the house, explained that the garret was used exclusively for the final testing of new instruments. Mr. Tomasi would go inside and play there alone for some time. Then he would come out, either with a smile on his face, which meant that he was satisfied with his work, or with a handful of firewood and broken strings; then it was best to stay away from him.

The inspector's efforts, with the help of the visibly distressed Mr. Umbertini, to find a farewell letter that his master might have left somewhere produced no results. This was not unusual. Those who did not really want to kill themselves, even though they actually did in the end, were the most frequent writers of such messages. Determined suicides did not find it necessary to interpret or justify their actions to the world, or to make their farewells.

By all appearances, Mr. Tomasi belonged to that category. Obviously the man had been firmly resolved to take this step, and had set about it without hesitation. It was a textbook case, clear and unambiguous. There was nothing more to investigate. The causes that had led the esteemed master violin-maker to commit suicide had not been established, but were of no interest to earthly justice. Let divine justice handle them, for it alone could know what had been on the suicide's mind.

Inspector Muratori ordered Mr. Umbertini to pack his things and leave the house so that it could be sealed pending probate. For a moment it seemed that the assistant wanted to make a comment or add something, about this or some other matter, but he held back. That was just as well. Everything had already been said, and the policeman could by no means help the poor man who was suddenly out on the street. But Inspector Muratori had seen far worse fates. This fellow would manage. A man who had learned the violin-maker's trade under maestro Tomasi need never be without an income. Such a recommendation would easily find him a job with another violin-maker, or he might even open his own shop.

The experienced policeman was rarely mistaken in his conclusions about people and their fates, but he was wrong this time. Mr. Umbertini neither looked for new employment nor tried to set up making violins on his own. With the savings he had been putting aside for years, he rented a small room in one of the narrow little streets off the square where he used to live. The rent was not high because the room was partially below street level and quite humid. This did not bother him unduly. In any event he only went there to sleep.

Mr. Umbertini spent most of his time in a tavern not far from the maestro's house. He had not frequented the place before, primarily because he hadn't been the least inclined to drink, but also because it had a bad reputation as a hangout for the *demi-monde*. Now neither reason mattered. He started to drink, first moderately, just enough to feel slightly intoxicated; then more and more. He hardly felt when he crossed the line and became addicted. The tavern only served cheap, low-quality wines and spirits that made Mr. Umbertini's head ache for a long time after waking in his dirty basement bed, but that did not deter him from going there every day.

At first the other tavern regulars were suspicious of the new patron and avoided his company. With his genteel manners and appearance, he was not part of their world. But as time passed and he became more and more like them in his person and behavior, they slowly started to warm to him. He no longer drank alone; they began to join him until finally all the places at his table were occupied almost all the time. They were a motley collection, and just a few months ago he certainly could not have imagined himself among them: frowning mercenaries from a regiment camped near the town, rotten-toothed and withered prostitutes, pickpockets on their way back from forays to the outdoor markets, tattered beggars, blemished and maimed.

Although Mr. Umbertini had no desire to talk about the suicide, with these people or with anyone else, the topic could not be avoided once their relations with the former assistant to the celebrated violin-maker, by now a thoroughly unkempt drunk, became familiar enough to remove their inhibitions. Unlike the police, who found it unnecessary to delve into what had forced the maestro to suicide, this mystery had never stopped intriguing prying minds, even in such a hole as this. Mr. Umbertini was subjected to a variety of approaches, from flattery through cajolery to threats, to get him to explain what had happened, but he withstood all such pressures without uttering a word. However, he could not avoid listening to the conjectures expounded by his fellow drinkers at the table in the tavern through the dense, stale cigarette smoke and sharp smell of sour wine.

One of the mercenaries, a man with a black patch over his left eye and a face full of scars, claimed he had heard from a reliable source that a legacy of madness in the family lay behind it all. Mr. Tomasi's paternal grandfather, a carpenter from a nearby village, had also taken his life, but in a far more painful way. When his mind had gone black he had shut himself in his workshop and started to stick every sharp tool he could find into his body. Not a single wound was fatal, but he died in prolonged agony, from blood loss, without uttering a single cry during that multiple, self-inflicted impalement. When his household forced their way into the workshop they beheld a horrible sight. The carpenter's body on the floor, arms outstretched like some horizontal crucifixion, resembled a hedgehog with thirty-three quills sticking out of it. His wife, who was five months pregnant, had a miscarriage and his only son, who was four at the time, was haunted his whole life by nightmares that caused him to wake up screaming.

Mr. Umbertini could easily have refuted this awful story, but he didn't. In the early days of his apprenticeship he had met the maestro's paternal grandfather. He had been a watch-mender here in town and had died in his sleep from heart failure at an advanced age. He had outlived his wife by several years, leaving seven children. The third of them, the first son after two daughters, was Mr. Tomasi's father, a cheerful and rather unruly man, certainly unburdened by dark stains from childhood, who died of suffocation on a fishbone, having been so incautious as to refill his mouth before he had finished laughing. Although not yet fully grown, the younger of his two sons, Alberto, who had inherited his mother's fine ear for music, took over his father's workshop where musical instruments were made and repaired. Not long afterward he narrowed his activities exclusively to making violins, and over time earned a reputation for his exceptional workmanship.

One of the prostitutes, whose original beauty could still be discerned despite her dilapidated state, though she was barely over thirty, had a completely different story. She had learned from someone imminently trustworthy that the cause of Mr. Tomasi's suicide was unrequited love. A traveling circus had camped near the town the previous summer and given performances on the square. Three musicians accompanied most of the acts, among them a young Gypsy woman who played the violin. At first the master violin-maker had complained about the noisy disturbance every evening in front of his house, but when he saw the girl he became more cordial.

He went to the window evening after evening and pretended to watch the events on the square, but never actually took his eyes off the young Gypsy. Finally, he went up to her at the end of a show, bringing the best instrument he had ever made. He invited her to his house and proposed she play this violin for him alone during the coming night, promising to pay her generously in return. The girl whispered briefly to one of the other two musicians, and then accepted. When she left Mr. Tomasi's house the next morning she was carrying the precious instrument wrapped in brown felt.

The next evening the master violin-maker waited impatiently on the terrace for the customary circus performance, but no one appeared. In the meantime the traveling show had decamped and continued on its way. Mr. Tomasi hired a horse at daybreak and set out in frantic search of them. He went to many of the nearby towns without finding a trace of the entertainers. The earth seemed to have swallowed them up. Completely crushed, he had finally been forced to abandon his search. He returned home, hoping time would heal his wounds and that he would somehow forget the beautiful violinist, but he couldn't get over her. He fell into a deeper and deeper depression, slowly losing the will and ability to make any more instruments. Finally, sunk in total despair, he decided to end his suffering.

The late master violin-maker's assistant knew from the outset that this story hadn't a grain of truth, but he didn't say so, among other things so as not to ruin the woman's pleasurable excitement as she recounted her tale. There was, in fact, a sad tale of love in the violin-maker's life, but it dated from his much younger days when he was still learning the skills of his trade. Love blossomed between him and a close cousin on his

142

mother's side. Although forbidden and clandestine, it was tempestuous, as often happens at that age. Who knows how things might have ended had illness not intervened? The girl came down with galloping tuberculosis and died only a few weeks later. He never became attached to a woman after that, although he did not renounce them. He tried to be as inconspicuous as possible when he slaked his urges, usually going to other towns for that purpose.

One of the pickpockets, a man with long, clever fingers but a face that was the very incarnation of innocence, swore on his honor that he had firsthand knowledge of the real reason Mr. Tomasi had killed himself. It was because of a huge gambling loss he had suffered. The violin-maker had been in the clutches of this obsession for some time, though no one knew anything about it, not even his assistant who lived under the same roof. A group of gamblers used to meet secretly at his house every Friday, going up to the garret from which he had finally jumped to his death. They would cover the window with the blanket from the bed so no one would suspect anything from outside, and then the game that had started by candlelight would often last till dawn.

As an honorable man, the violin-maker had been convinced that his companions were his equals in integrity. He had had not the slightest inkling he had fallen into a network of shrewd and unscrupulous cheats. At first they bet small amounts, and he mostly won. Then Lady Luck suddenly turned her back on him.

He started losing not only his money but his common sense. He agreed to increase the bets in the futile hope he would win back what he had lost, but he only sank deeper and deeper into debt. When his cash and valuables disappeared, he started to write IOUs. First he lost his large estate in the country, then his house in town. He still managed to hold up somehow, but when the cards took away the last of his expensive instruments, he realized he had hit rock bottom. In the end he caught on, realizing he had been the victim of a trick, but there was no turning back. Unable to live with the thought that his violins were in the hands of cunning thieves, he sentenced himself to the ultimate punishment.

It was pure invention, of course, but Mr. Umbertini still made no comment. Gambling organized every Friday, however discreetly, would never have escaped his attention. Moreover, Mr. Tomasi had never had a country estate to lose. Far more important than these details, however, was the fact that gambling was the last vice to which the maestro would have succumbed; without ever being touched by it personally, he had experienced the grievous consequences of this addiction.

The violin-maker's older brother, Roberto Tomasi, had been a regular attendee at large casinos since he was a young man. He had left his share of their father's inheritance in them long ago, but for some time afterward continued to gratify this irresistible vice thanks to his brother's generous support. Alberto had shown a strange compassion for Roberto's weakness, agreeing to pay his gambling debts, until one day he refused to give him the large amount he had come for. Thereupon Roberto had, in a fit of rage, seized a newly finished violin and smashed it against the wall. The two brothers never saw each other again after that, even though the older brother had sent many letters of apology and had even gone to plead at his younger brother's door.

A crippled beggar, who claimed to be the illegitimate son of a duke, patiently listened to all three stories and announced confidently that none of them was true. The master violin-maker had not committed suicide at all, whatever people thought. He did not jump from the window, he was thrown out of it. There was a third eyewitness to this tragedy as well as the two baker's men. He was a beggar who had left town in a hurry immediately after the fateful event, fearing what he had seen, and pausing only long enough to confide in his lame friend.

The beggar had spent the night on the square and was sleeping under some stairs when he was awakened at daybreak by banging from somewhere above. He looked around drowsily, then realized the noise was coming from the open window in the garret of the violin-maker's house. It seemed as if someone was trying to break something in there, but he could see nothing from below. Then everything quieted down and a brief silence reigned. Just as the two baker's boys arrived in the square from a side street, each carrying baskets full of freshly baked bread and rolls, the terrified maestro appeared at the window. He held tightly onto the frame, trying to resist whoever was pushing him from behind. It was a silent struggle, which was why the young men were completely unaware of it. They crossed the square, unsuspecting among the pigeons, chatting in low voices.

The unrelenting pressure on the maestro's back grew stronger and stronger until his resistance yielded. As if hurled by a huge hand, he flew out of the window and plunged helplessly toward the pavement, still without uttering a sound. Behind him, however, the window was not empty as it would have been had he jumped of his own free will. A terrifying figure appeared for just an instant, curdling the blood in the observer's veins as he lay hidden under the stairs. It disappeared at once, but that fleeting look was enough for the beggar to recognize it beyond all doubt. He remained hidden for quite some time, not daring to move. It was only after the police inspector had completed his investigation and the dead man's body was removed that the beggar mustered the courage to come out.

It should surprise no one, the lame beggar concluded didactically, that Mr. Tomasi finally fell victim to the Tempter. Anyone who pledges his soul to the Devil for the sake of some vain and evanescent acclaim must be assured that the Devil will get his due—sooner or later. The master violin-maker had no reason to complain; he had gloried for many years in his reputation as the unsurpassed creator of magnificent violins, though it was clear to everyone that such talent could not be natural.

That was when Mr. Umbertini was first tempted to contribute a comment of his own. Unlike the other stories, this one was at least partially credible. The storyteller himself had probably been the eyewitness on the square that morning, rather than this nameless friend who had so conveniently disappeared. Most likely he was reluctant to admit as much for fear of being questioned by the police, but he had given too many convincing details for one who was merely recounting another's experience. The supplementary elements he had invented were understandable in the circumstances; without them his story would not have been exciting enough for the listeners in the tavern. On the other hand, although he could not have known, they were not completely unfounded. Nonetheless, the ex-assistant decided once again not to say anything, principally because of his unwillingness to enter into the inevitable discussion about this aspect of the maestro's accident, for the secret at its heart greatly surpassed his own understanding.

He might never have spoken of it at all had his hand not been forced by an extraordinary chain of events. The vagabonds and good-for-nothings who kept him company in the tavern started to lose interest in the violin-maker's suicide as it became clear they would get nothing out of his former assistant. They also found the man himself less and less interesting, since he passed most of his time sunk in gloomy silence, concentrating on the bottle. They gradually started to drop away, leaving him alone finally at the table. At last only the large, bearded innkeeper sometimes exchanged a word or two with him.

One rainy day in late autumn, Mr. Umbertini arrived at the

tavern early, while there were still no other guests. He sat at a small table with two chairs in the corner, close to the hearth, and the innkeeper, without asking and giving just a brief nod, brought him three bottles of red wine and a glass. He peered briefly at his customer's thin, unshaven face, inflamed eyes and red nose, but said nothing. The innkeeper couldn't care less about the appearance of those who frequented his establishment as long as they had money to pay for what they ordered. It was not his job to warn immoderate drunks that every new glass only shortened what little life they had left. He picked up the coins that Mr. Umbertini put on the table without a word and slipped them into the deep pocket under his stained apron, then went behind the bar.

Mr. Umbertini was already halfway through the second bottle when new guests started to appear in the tavern. They were certainly not those he was accustomed to seeing there. First a little boy came in. He could not have been more than six or seven years old, but he went up to the largest table, sat at the head of it, took out a piece of paper and pencil from somewhere, bowed his head and started to write something in a tiny script. From time to time he took out a handkerchief and held it briefly to his nose. After him came a middle-aged woman holding a bunch of scrolls under her arm. She sat next to the boy, unrolled a scroll and became engrossed in reading. The refined older man who soon joined them brought a snow-white cat with him. He stroked it gently in his lap, whispering in its ear. The older woman who next arrived stood at the entrance, looking in bewilderment first at the innkeeper and then at the master violin-maker's assistant as though she had seen ghosts. She sat down stiffly on one of the three unoccupied chairs and put her muff on the table in front of her without removing her hands. The man who came in after her was a painter. As soon as he joined the others he opened a large sketching block, took a stick of charcoal and began sketching in brisk, rough strokes. Finally, the last to arrive was a rather casually dressed man with dishevelled gray hair. He rummaged through his pockets for a few moments, finally found a piece of chalk and without the least hesitation began to write on the uncovered wooden table, erasing something here and there with the leather-patched elbow of his jacket.

The sight of six such strangers at the big table was extremely unusual in this establishment. During all the months Mr. Umbertini had spent in the tavern he had never seen anyone even slightly resembling them. But what seemed to him almost as unbelievable was the fact that the innkeeper paid them absolutely no attention. He, who took great pains that no guest ever be left even momentarily without a glass or plate on the table in front of him, who kept an eye on empty glasses in order to fill them at once, and never recoiled from showing the door to anyone who contemplated sitting inside for free, had not even approached these dignified guests, though they clearly promised a good tab. Instead, he went up to the assistant's table, waved at the other chair with the dirty rag he constantly wore over his arm, and sat down.

He came straight to the point. He maintained that he knew why Mr. Tomasi had killed himself—a most unexpected statement as he had never taken part in the conversations on the subject. He had seemed totally uninterested, just idly listening to the stories told by others. The master violin-maker, the innkeeper now asserted, had wanted to make a perfect violin. He had invested years of effort and everything indicated he was on the right track. Unfortunately, no human hands, not even the most gifted, are able to reach perfection. Although appearing perfect in every way, the violin was nonetheless not divine, as he had hoped. When he realized this after testing it that morning, the violin-maker understood there was only one way out of this defeat, and he took it.

This time Mr. Umbertini could hold back no longer. Had the innkeeper's story simply been wrong, he certainly would not have reacted, gliding over it as he had the others. But he had found one essential aspect of this story deeply offensive, and he alone could now stand up to defend the maestro's besmirched honor. That was a debt he owed his teacher, and it took precedence over the pledge the assistant had made to himself never to reveal what had happened in the garret.

The innkeeper had been right, although Mr. Umbertini could not even imagine how that simple and greedy seller of bad wine could have found out something the maestro had kept secret even from his faithful pupil. For eighteen years, with endless devotion and patience, he had indeed been working on a perfect violin. It was only toward the end that the assistant finally understood what lay hidden behind the violin-maker's periodic retreats to the highest room in the house. He would stay locked inside for hours, though he had taken no instrument with him to test, and no one dared disturb him.

The innkeeper, however, was wrong when he said, with an edge of malice in his voice, that the master violin-maker had been unsuccessful in his efforts. Sneaking up to the garret on that fateful morning when the unique violin was given its final test, Mr. Umbertini heard the sound of divine harmony for the first and only time in his life. Even though the closed door dampened the music, the magic of that experience had been so powerful that he had felt compelled to stay close to the maestro's house instead of going somewhere else, where he might hope to enjoy a more useful and fulfilling life—despite his awareness that he would never again be given an opportunity to hear it.

Mr. Umbertini knew the question the innkeeper would ask next, just as he knew that he had no answer. If the maestro had truly created a perfect violin, what had happened to it? Or to its remains, if the crashing that the beggar on the square had heard meant that the maestro had broken it? (Although why would he do such a thing to his masterpiece?) When the inspector had forced the door, nothing had been found inside: neither a whole instrument nor its wreckage. So the garret must have possessed a secret entrance, concluded the cunning innkeeper, which the assistant had used before the inspector's arrival in order to remove all traces.

This was a logical assumption that offered an explanation for both possibilities: that the violin had been perfect and that it hadn't been. Its only defect was that it was incorrect. There was no secret entrance to the highest room in the building. When he finally entered the garret with the inspector, the assistant encountered his second wonder of that morning. Although the instrument had to be there, and in one piece, it was not. And the fact that it should have been in one piece constituted the first wonder.

As Mr. Umbertini stood in front of the door, still dazzled by the music that had just ended, he suddenly heard something inside that terrified him. He was quite familiar with that sound. The crashing could mean only one thing: the master violinmaker was destroying his life's work! But why? Not knowing what else to do, the assistant quickly dropped to his knees and tried to peer in through the keyhole. Had there been no key in the lock, he could have seen more, but even this way he was able to catch at least partial sight of the maestro's crazed figure as he swung the violin, holding it by the neck. He hit it against whatever he came across: the table, chair back, bed frame, walls.

Even though the full force of his unbridled rage went into it, the instrument was not so much as scratched. The violin steadfastly resisted all his attempts to shatter it, remaining untouched, as though he were merely swinging it through the air. When he threw it to the floor and started to jump on it, again without causing any damage, he finally collapsed, sat on the edge of the bed, thrust his head in his hands and stayed there unmoving for a while. And then he got up slowly, went to the large window, grabbed the frame, remained in that position a few moments, then let go and simply leaned forward. The dumbfounded assistant took his eye off the keyhole and slid to the floor next to the door. It was not until the inspector banged the door knocker at the entrance to the house that he was startled out of his paralysis.

The innkeeper shook his head. Of all the stories he had heard, he said, this one seemed the most far-fetched. Thank heavens Mr. Umbertini had not told it to the police, because that would surely have focused suspicion on himself. He personally still thought the only true explanation lay in the secret entrance. As far as the noise was concerned, it didn't have to come from breaking the violin; rather its maker might have banged the furniture around him in frustration over his failure, as people do when they are infuriated.

In any case, the innkeeper concluded, after the master violin-maker jumped through the window, Mr. Umbertini had gone into the garret and stowed the instrument somewhere. He had waited for the situation to calm down, then sold it under the counter. The violin might not have been perfect according to Mr. Tomasi's criteria, but the seller certainly would have received a pretty sum for it that would enable him to lead a comfortable life. For example, he could amuse himself at the tavern day after day without having to work. But Mr. Umbertini had no need to worry. The innkeeper certainly would not turn him in. What benefit would that bring him? He would only be losing a regular customer who had never asked for credit.

Seeing there was nothing more to say, he returned to the bar. He started to wipe glasses idly, continuing to neglect the six visitors at the other table. They sat there briefly, involved in their preoccupations, and then, as though at an invisible signal, stood up and left the tavern together, offended no doubt at being so rudely ignored. Mr. Umbertini watched them leave, and then, as though remembering something, quickly got up and headed after them, leaving almost a bottle and a half of wine, paid for but not drunk. He was never seen in there again.

For a while stories were concocted in the tavern regarding his disappearance. It was heard on great authority that thieves had slaughtered him and thrown him into the river, that he had left for the New World to seek his fortune, that he had opened his own workshop in another town, and that he had come down with leprosy and was now living out the miserable remainder of his days in an asylum on some island. Only the sober innkeeper, who was not to be cheated, knew they were all fabrications and that, as usual, the simplest explanation was the soundest: the late master violin-maker's assistant had fled, fearing someone might denounce him to the police once he had spent all of his dishonestly acquired money.

Photograph by Imre Szabo

A truly unique author whose work bends trusted concepts in a seductively ordinary manner, Zoran Živković has been compared to such luminaries as Italo Calvino, Franz Kafka, and Stanislew Lem. His work has been broadcast on BBC radio, produced by Belgrade Studio B television, optioned for film, and published in eleven countries; by the end of 2006 six more countries will have joined that list. He has been nominated for several awards and received the World Fantasy Award in 2003 for his mosaic novel *The Library*.

His mosaic novels *Steps Through the Mist* and *Impossible Encounters* will appear in the United States and Canada in 2007 and 2008.

The author was born in Belgrade, former Yugoslavia, in 1948. In 1973 he graduated from the University of Belgrade's Department of General Literature with a degree in literature; he received his master's degree in 1979 and his doctorate in 1982 from the same school.

He lives in Belgrade, Serbia, with his wife Mia, their twin sons Uroš and Andreja, and their four cats.

Find out more about

Seven Touches of Music

and author Zoran Živković
at www.aiopublishing.com

Reviews
Author interview
Write your own review
Direct email link to the author

Order another copy of this book online at
www.aiopublishing.com for free shipping
and fast fulfillment of your order.

Or to order by mail, please send a request and
check or money order for $23.00 plus $3.00 for
shipping (South Carolina residents please
add applicable sales tax) to:

aio

Aio Publishing Co., LLC
P. O. Box 30788
Charleston, SC 29417
USA

Please also consider our friends to the north...
OnSpec is the Canadian magazine of the fantastic,
nominated many times over for the Hugo Award
(Best Semi-Pro Magazine). Mention this page
to them and receive a free back issue!